Dear Reader,

I've loved dogs all my life, and when I started to research this book and discovered just how much dogs do within both the United States and Australian armed forces, I was blown away. These courageous dogs are taught how to detect explosives and, along with their handlers, save the lives of so many soldiers. These dogs ask for little more than love, shelter and food, and in return they are the most faithful and tireless of workers.

Their handlers are also incredibly brave and courageous. They are the most elite of soldiers—men capable of the highest level of service within the armed forces—and the love they have for their four-legged comrades is second to none. Their dogs rarely leave their side, and they treat them with all the respect and love they deserve.

I hope you enjoy this story of love and second chances, and of course the love of man's best friend—the humble dog. In this book you will meet not only the hero, but one of the hero's closest friends, too, and I'm pleased to tell you that there will be a second book to follow.

If you enjoy this story, I'd love to hear from you. I also encourage you to visit my website and find out more about my past and upcoming releases.

Soraya Lane

The Returning Hero

Soraya Lane

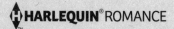

HARLEQUIN® ROMANCE

Recycling programs
for this product may
not exist in your area.

ISBN-13: 978-0-373-74280-6

THE RETURNING HERO

First North American Publication 2014

Copyright © 2014 by Soraya Lane

Printed in U.S.A.

www.Harlequin.com

Writing for the Harlequin® Romance line is truly a dream come true for **Soraya Lane**. An avid book reader and writer since her childhood, Soraya describes becoming a published author as "the best job in the world," and hopes to be writing heartwarming, emotional romances for many years to come.

Soraya lives with her own real-life hero on a small farm in New Zealand, surrounded by animals and with an office overlooking a field where their horses graze.

For more information about Soraya and her upcoming releases, visit her at her website, www.sorayalane.com, her blog, www.sorayalane.blogspot.com, or follow her at www.facebook.com/SorayaLaneAuthor.

Recent books by Soraya Lane

PATCHWORK FAMILY IN THE OUTBACK*
MISSION: SOLDIER TO DADDY
THE SOLDIER'S SWEETHEART
THE NAVY SEAL'S BRIDE
BACK IN THE SOLDIER'S ARMS
RODEO DADDY
THE ARMY RANGER'S RETURN
SOLDIER ON HER DOORSTEP

Bellaroo Creek!

These and other titles by Soraya Lane are available in ebook format from www.Harlequin.com

For Hamish & Mackenzie. I'm so fortunate that you both share my love of dogs!

In Dogs We Trust

The unofficial motto of the soldiers within the Explosive Detection Dog Service

CHAPTER ONE

BRETT PALMER LEANED against the door of his vehicle. Visiting had seemed like a great idea before he'd left home, but now he was here… turning up unannounced wasn't so easy. Perhaps if he'd planned what he was going to say, had a good reason for not touching base with her before now, but he'd just jumped in the car and decided to chance it.

He sucked back a big breath and forced himself to walk forward. He'd known Jamie Mattheson for years, so it wasn't like she'd get a shock to see him, but still. It wasn't as if he'd ever spent time with her on her own, either.

Brett swallowed the memories, refusing to go back in time, and jogged the last few steps to the front door. He knocked. No one answered. There wasn't even so much as a shuffle from inside. Brett knocked again.

He could either get in his car and leave, or head around back to see if she was there. The sun was already out in full force, typical of Sydney at this time of year, and he had more than a hunch that she could be out in the garden.

Brett stepped back down and walked around the side of the house. It was looking nice, but then he knew Sam had painted the weatherboards before he'd left for their last tour, had made sure he'd done all the maintenance so Jamie had nothing to worry about while he was gone. He'd put money on it that she'd prefer the house to be falling down around her if it meant she could go back in time and have her husband back.

Brett pushed the side gate open and looked around the corner. *There she was*. Standing with her hands on her hips, like something was really frustrating her. Then he saw the something, sitting in front of her, alert, nose pointed in the air.

Bear. She had Sam's dog. How the hell had she ended up with Bear so soon?

"Jamie," he called out, not wanting to startle her but not wanting to be caught staring at her, either.

The dog had given up sitting patiently and was now barking and thundering toward him. He'd been his best mate's dog, but right now he was protecting his new owner, and Brett wasn't exactly game to take the massive canine on.

"Bear, it's me," he called out, as the black dog hurtled toward him. "Bear! It's okay, boy."

The dog slowed, still looking protective, but Brett was comfortable that he was no longer about to be attacked.

"Brett? What are you doing here?"

Jamie was suddenly rushing across the lawn to him, arms outstretched.

"Hey, sweetheart." He held his own arms out, one eye on the dog, until she threw herself against him.

Brett held her tight, holding on to her like his life depended upon it. He'd been best man at their wedding, vacationed with them, had dinner at their house…and now he was comforting a widow.

"It's so good to see you." Jamie stepped

back, but she held on to his hands, firmly, like she'd never let go.

Brett looked into her eyes, saw tears there that she was bravely holding in check. This woman had been his best friend's wife, and he'd never, ever wanted to be in this position. He was just grateful that he hadn't been the one to tell her the news when it had happened.

"You've got Bear." He knew he was stating the obvious but he still couldn't believe it.

He turned half his attention back to the dog, who was keeping a close eye on them.

"And I have no idea what to do with him," she admitted, stepping back and letting go of Brett. Jamie had her hands back on her hips as she stared at the dog. "I'm doing my best, but he's, I don't know, smarter than me, I guess. We're not communicating that well."

Brett dropped to his haunches, eye level with the canine. "Hey, Bear. Remember me, bud?" The dog let out a low whine, looking up at Jamie then back to him again. "I know you do. Come here."

Bear slowly walked over to him and sat down on Brett's feet. He gave him a scratch, liking that the dog had accepted him. God only knew they'd spent enough time together when he was serving.

"I'll teach you everything I can, Jamie. He's a pretty special dog, but he's used to certain commands and lots of them."

She laughed. "Yeah, sometimes I wondered if Sam thought he was more special than me. Probably showed off photos of him to everyone and forgot all about his wife."

Brett reached for her, took her hand again as he stood to full height. "You know that's not true. You meant everything to Sam." He chuckled. "To be honest, we all had to tell him to knock it off most of the time. He talked about you *way* too often."

She laughed, gripping his hand tight. "You always were the charmer."

He put his arm around her, needing to hold her, to show her how much he cared. "I miss him, Jamie. I miss him so bad that I can't…" Brett blew out a breath, dropping his chin to the top of her head. "I just needed you to know that I'm here for you. It's taken me a while, but I'm back now."

Jamie looped her arm around his waist

and steered them toward the house. "How about we have brunch?"

"Here?"

"Yeah, why not," she said. "Besides, I haven't had anyone to make pancakes for in a while."

Brett signaled to the dog to follow them, and walked behind Jamie as she went into the house. She was dressed in a tiny pair of cut-off denim shorts and a loose-fitting T-shirt, and he wished she were covered up. She was his friend's widow. She was beautiful. Her legs were so long and tanned.... He forced his eyes to the sky. *Jamie was Sam's wife.* Just because he'd loved her from the moment he'd met her, thought she was the most caring, gorgeous woman he'd ever spent time with, didn't mean it was okay to start giving in to his feelings now.

Sam had been gone only a little over six months. He'd been his best friend. And Jamie was his widow, he reminded himself again.

But deep down, Brett knew exactly why he'd put off coming for so long.

Jamie hadn't stopped moving since they'd walked inside. She couldn't. Because if she stopped even for a second, she'd either start crying or throw her arms around Brett and never let him go.

Having him here was unexpected, unusual, and yet exactly what she needed all at the same time. Since Sam had been gone, she'd had an emptiness inside of her that had ached every single day, but seeing Brett...? It was like the pain was finally easing. Because she could talk to Brett about her husband, really talk about him, and he made her feel like Sam could still walk through the front door, hassling Brett for chatting her up like he usually did. Jamie took a deep breath.

"Maple syrup?" she asked.

He laughed. "Yes, ma'am."

Jamie flipped a pancake and turned around to look at the man seated at her counter. He looked like he always did—handsome and tanned—but there was something different about him now. Something she couldn't pinpoint, except for maybe a hint of unhappiness that kept crossing his face, that made his smile never quite reach his eyes like it once had. There was so much she wanted to ask him, but she wanted to wait until the time was right.

"So tell me how you ended up with Bear?" Brett asked.

She smiled at the dog lying near her feet. He might be hard to communicate with, but he sure was loyal and she loved him for that.

"The detection dog unit contacted me, told me that he had to be retired after the accident, and they wanted to offer him to me first." She shook her head, turning her attention back to her pancakes. "Sam loved him so much, so I couldn't say no. And it is kind of nice having the company, even if we haven't quite figured each other out yet. He's only been here a few weeks because he had to be in quarantine for a while."

She knew Brett had lost his dog in the same explosion that had killed her husband, that he probably wasn't ready to go there yet, but...

"I know I should have come by sooner, Jamie, it's just..." Brett's voice trailed off.

Jamie held up her hand. It seemed like they were both struggling to find the right words. "No apology necessary. We just do what we have to do to cope, right?"

He nodded, looked grateful that he didn't have to explain himself. Instead of asking him anything further, she flipped the last pancake and placed it in front of him, adding it to the stack.

"Looks good enough to eat," he said, grinning as he poured syrup over them.

Jamie sat down beside him, reaching for the coffeepot she'd left just out of reach. It seemed right having Brett here, even if it was just the two of them, because being alone these last six months, she'd started to forget the person she was, the happy, easygoing person she'd always been. Brett was making her remember how nice it had always been to open their home to friends.

She chanced a quick glance at him, wishing she could resist but unable to. When they'd first met, Brett was dating another woman, and then when he was single she'd already been seeing Sam. *His best friend.* Just because they'd been attracted to one another before didn't mean anything, she knew that, but she had a notion that she should be feeling guilty, shouldn't feel so comfortable in his presence.

"Do you still have your house here?"

Jamie watched as he finished his mouthful before setting his fork back down on the plate. "I decided to put it on the market a while back, and it sold while I was deployed."

"Oh." She hadn't known. "So where are you staying?" She'd been wanting to get in touch with him for months, had presumed he was away again, because he hadn't even been able to make it back for Sam's service.

"I've been at a recuperation clinic. My leg was burned pretty bad when the..." His sentence trailed off. "It's kept me away for a while, then I traveled around for a bit to come to grips with everything, and I only just arrived in yesterday."

She swallowed, taking a deep breath before she asked a question that needed to be voiced. "You're staying in a hotel, aren't you? You only came back here to see me."

Brett looked guilty. "You were Sam's wife. I could only stay away for so long. He'd want me to look out for you, Jamie. You know that. He even asked me as much."

Unspoken words hung between them, words that would never be braved by either of them. Because before it had just been flirting. Now that Sam was gone... It was too soon for either of them, wasn't something that could ever happen. But it didn't mean she wanted Brett to leave, and it didn't mean that he was here for any other reason than because he loved her for being Sam's wife.

"I want you to know that I'm here, no matter what you need, okay?"

Jamie stared at him, raised one eyebrow as she looked into his eyes. "You really want to be here for me? To help me?"

He nodded. "Of course."

"Then help me with Bear," she said. "Turn me into a worthy owner of the dog who meant the world to my husband."

Brett was playing with his fork, looking at the half-eaten breakfast on his plate.

"You're sure you want me hanging around?" he asked. "I mean, you don't have to say that just because…"

Jamie reached for his hand, squeezed it and stared straight into Brett's eyes. "You weren't just his friend, you were mine, too," she confessed. "I've missed you guys—you, Sam and Logan. I miss you all. I didn't just lose my husband, I lost having you two here all the time, too."

Brett grunted. "Bet Logan's been better at staying in touch."

She shook her head. "He's phoned me a couple of times, but I haven't seen him, either. It's been—" Jamie shrugged "—weird. But he did say he was back in town soon, so maybe he's back now?"

Brett looked surprised, but she didn't say anything. He went back to eating his pancakes and so did she.

"Well, if you need help with Bear, I'm here," he said. "How about we start with a few basics today, and I'll come past tomorrow and we can take him out to a park or something."

Jamie stood up to clear their plates. "That sounds like a good plan," she told him.

A niggle in her mind was telling her she should have asked Brett to stay, that her husband would have been horrified that his best buddy was paying to stay at a hotel, but she wasn't ready for that. Wasn't ready for a man to be sleeping in her home, under her roof—a man who wasn't her husband, even if she did hate being on her own at night. Being alone…it took her back to her childhood, brought the ice-cold fear back, and she hated that as much as the reality of waking up without Sam beside her.

And if she were honest with herself, she was feeling nervous about being with Brett too much, just the two of them. They'd always flirted, it was just how he'd always been with her, but back then she'd also been in love with her husband, which meant their joking had always been nothing more than fun. Now?

She just had to take one day at a time. Having Brett here was better than being on her own, and she knew it was what Sam would have wanted. Even if she was having feelings about Brett that he wouldn't approve of.

CHAPTER TWO

BRETT DIDN'T KNOW what he'd expected, but being with Jamie was...different. He always knew it wasn't going to be the same without Sam, and he was pleased he was here, but it didn't make it easy.

Thank God they had Bear to deal with. He would have felt weird coming over again without a good reason, without a purpose to help her.

"So did Sam ever teach you any of his commands?"

Jamie shook her head. He could tell she loved the dog, and it looked as if the canine reciprocated—the trouble was plain simple communication. Bear was sitting faithfully beside Jamie, and her hand had fallen to the top of his head, which told him that there was no reason they weren't going to form a good team. They just weren't in sync yet, and that's what he was going to help her with.

"The thing with this dog is that he's extremely easy to teach, so long as you make your commands and actions clear and consistent," Brett told her. "You don't have to be Sam, but you do have to understand how he learns."

"Do you mean like how they need to be rewarded by play?"

Brett grinned. "Exactly. This dog was chosen for the dog detection unit because when we tested him as a youngster, his commitment to a game of ball was unwavering."

"So I need to play with him?" she asked, staring down at the dog.

"Yeah, you need to play with him, and you need to let him be with you all the time, because that's how Sam treated him whenever they were together."

Jamie was laughing and he loved seeing her happy, as if for a moment they were both here for any reason other than because of what had happened—that they were just two friends catching up under the sun, like old times.

"You guys always act so tough, but when it comes to your dogs, you're like marshmallows."

"It's part of the bonding process, you know that," he told her, pretending to be offended. "And we *are* tough, I'll have you know."

"Yeah, that's what you all tell each other, but really? You're just lonely when you're away and want a warm body in your bed to snuggle up to."

Brett laughed, unable to help himself. "How did you figure us all out so fast, huh?"

Jamie held up her hand to shield her face from the sun. "So are we just going to start with the basics?"

He nodded. "Why don't we run through sit, stay and heel, then I'll teach you how to play with a ninety-pound canine. Sound good?"

The smile she gave him made him drop his gaze, focus on the dog instead, because he was walking a dangerous line between helping out a friend's widow and wanting to be here because he'd always liked Jamie and still did.

And if he were honest with himself, it's

why he'd taken so long to come back. It hadn't just been about his injury, it hadn't just been because he was struggling to come to terms with losing his best human friend *and* his canine best friend, it was because when it came to Jamie, he didn't trust himself. He could have all the best intentions in the world, but without Sam here, he was screwed.

Jamie watched as Brett moved across the grass, Bear running along beside him and then bounding ahead to catch the ball.

"You just need to have fun with him," Brett called out. "Let him know you love playing just as much as he does."

She couldn't help but laugh at them as they charged around her small lawn.

"It's not about the space, it's the quality of time you spend with him. He wants you to guide him, to be his leader and his equal, too. He will always look to you for direction, because that's what he's been trained to do."

"So in other words he wants me to be his wife?"

They both laughed and she watched as Brett nodded to the dog to follow him.

"You must miss your dog," she said, wishing she could take the words back the moment they left her lips.

Brett's mouth fixed in a hard line, his jaw clamped before he took a visibly deep breath. "Every goddamn day," he told her, running a hand through his short brown hair. "Teddy hardly left my side in four years. It was like he always knew what I was thinking before I'd even thought it myself. And then…"

Jamie felt like her breath had died in her throat, her lungs refusing to cooperate. The day Teddy had died had been the day Sam had died, too.

They stared at one another. She watched as Brett swallowed. Neither of them wanted to talk about that day, because somehow Brett had made it home and her husband and Brett's dog had been killed. She wished the comment had never come out of her mouth, but it wasn't like she could take it back.

"Have you had any ongoing veterinary care for Bear? I'm hoping after all he did for the army that he's on a full pension."

He'd changed the subject but only just, although she wasn't complaining.

"When I collected him he was pretty much healed, on the outside at least," Jamie told him. "He had a bandaged paw still and lots of missing or singed fur, but they made sure he was almost back to health before letting me take him. And they seemed to look after him pretty well when he was quarantined."

"I was the one who carried him back to the truck," Brett told her, his voice low. "He managed to come toward me, but the ringing in his ears must have been as bad as it was in mine because he couldn't even walk in a straight line, and his paws and legs were badly burned. There was no part of me that could have tried to get away without helping him, and it was like he wanted to do the same for me."

Jamie refused to look away, no matter how uncomfortable the conversation was making her, because she knew how hard it must have been for Brett to talk about what had happened, even just a little.

"I can't believe you even managed to lift him, after what had happened to you," she said softly.

Brett dropped to his haunches and slung

his arm around the dog. "If it hadn't been for this boy," he said, stroking the dog's fur as he spoke, "everyone in that truck would have died that day. It wasn't until I collapsed that I realized why my body was burning so bad, what a mess my leg was, and then I passed out from the pain and shock. Bear was braver than any of us."

Brett was staring past her now, and Jamie didn't want to make him uncomfortable. It was so nice having him here, having a familiar face to chat to, that she wanted to make sure he stayed for the afternoon.

"What do you say we take him for a walk?" she suggested.

Brett smiled, clearly relieved she'd changed the subject completely.

"Do you usually take him out?" he asked.

She grimaced. "It's not that I don't want to, but he's kind of massive and I'm worried I won't be able to control him if we come across another dog or something."

Brett shook his head. "Did that husband of yours teach you *nothing* about this dog?"

She laughed. "No, because it was like they shared the same brain! Bear just did what Sam wanted him to do, like they had some silent communication thing going on, and he went everywhere with him so it wasn't like I was ever in sole charge."

Brett sighed. "Fair call." He followed her inside and stood back as she locked the doors. "How about you tell me what you'd like to do with him?"

She checked the side door was locked before gathering Bear's lead from a drawer and facing Brett.

"I guess I want to be able to walk down for a coffee and sit without worrying how to handle him if there's another big dog coming toward us. And walk through the park, throw a ball for him and know he'll come back when he's off the leash, that sort of thing."

Brett opened the front door and held it open for her, waiting as she clipped the leash to Bear's collar.

"He's too well-trained to have a fight with another dog, and he will never, *ever* chase a ball and not bring it back to you. It's why he made the squad in the first place."

"Were you with Sam the day he chose him?"

Brett shook his head. "No, but I remember

him being so excited that he'd finally found the perfect partner. Bear was with a family who loved him, but they were moving overseas and had put him up for adoption. When Sam went to see him, he tested him out with a ball and he knew straight away that the black giant was going to be his sidekick."

They fell into a comfortable rhythm, walking side by side.

"Is it okay to talk about him?" Brett asked, his voice an octave lower.

The question took her by surprise. "Yes." They walked for a bit more before she continued. "I mean, it's hard, it's always hard, but it's nice talking about him with you."

"I half expect him to be at the house when we get back," Brett said with a smile. "Waiting to give me a telling off about hanging out with his wife."

"Yeah." Jamie was smiling, too, but it was bittersweet. "I guess I'd become so used to him going away on tours, so for me it just seems like this has just been an especially long one. Like I'm just waiting for him to fly home and pick up where we left off." It had been the same when her dad had never come home from deployment—like one day he'd just walk through the door again and everything would go back to normal.

"If it's too hard having me here…"

"No," she blurted. "Having you here is the only good thing that's happened to me in a long while, so please don't think you're making me uncomfortable. It's the complete opposite."

Brett was pleased she wanted him here, but every time they talked about Sam made him feel plain weird for being with Jamie, just the two of them. Lucky they had the dog as a distraction, because it meant they had something to focus on other than the fact that nothing was like it had been the last time they'd seen one another.

"So you just give him a gentle reminder if he walks ahead of you by pulling the lead back," he told her, closing his hand over it and showing her, "and telling him to heel, but you're probably not going to need to do that very often."

Brett didn't move his hand when Jamie's brushed past it, fingers almost closing over his before she realized. It was stupid—they'd touched plenty in the past—but having her warm skin against his reminded him of all the reasons why he shouldn't have been here. Because there had been a time when he'd wished he'd asked Jamie out, before she'd met Sam, and they were dangerous thoughts to be remembering now that she was his friend's widow.

"Brett, I don't want to bring up what happened again, but I need to ask you one question."

He cleared his throat and turned to face her. "Shoot." So long as he didn't have to relive what had happened again, he'd tell her what she needed to know. Those memories caught up on him enough without voluntarily calling on them.

"I keep thinking about the army sending Bear back, once they'd made the decision to retire him. Is it normal for them to care for a dog like that, even though their career is over, and then pay to send them home?"

Brett couldn't help smiling at her. Trust Jamie to have figured out that it wasn't exactly protocol, especially when the handler was no longer alive and able to fight for his dog.

"Let's just say that me and the other boys

put a fair amount of pressure on our superiors to make sure Bear had a good retirement. I didn't know he'd be given back to you, but there aren't that many dogs in the world capable of what he did on a daily basis, and it wasn't exactly a tough call to send him home a hero."

Jamie reached out to him, took him completely by surprise as her hand stayed in place on his shoulder.

"Well then I guess I owe you a pretty big thanks," she said, throwing him a smile that made him want to look away, because that smile had always teased him and he didn't want to think about her like that, not now. "It means a lot to have him here, even if I'm kind of hopeless at the whole business of looking after a dog."

Brett fought not to shrug her hand off, and was pleased when it just dropped away.

"So which café are we going to?"

"Skinny latte?"

Jamie looked up. "How did you guess?"

He chuckled and ordered, before peering into the cabinet with her. "And I'm also guessing that you want something sweet. Maybe the chocolate peppermint slice?"

Jamie kept staring at the rows of food, trying to ignore the slice so she wasn't completely predictable. In the end she gave in to her sweet tooth. "Okay, how about we share a piece?"

She walked back outside to where they'd left Bear, not liking the idea of just tying him up and leaving him beside a table.

"He's fine," Brett said, pulling her chair out for her and then taking the seat opposite.

"I can see that. It just seems foreign to me," she told him.

"This dog won't let you down. Trust me. His manners will be better than most of the people in here."

Jamie rolled her eyes, but she knew he was probably right. And she also knew that Brett pulling her chair out for her was the kind of gentlemanly thing that not many guys did anymore. Her husband had, so she was used to it, and she liked being treated like a woman.

Brett's mobile rang and he punched a button to silence it before answering and mouthing *sorry* to her. Jamie touched Bear's head, stroking his fur, not looking at Brett. But she couldn't help but take notice of what he was saying. The fact that it was Logan, her husband's other best buddy, made her want to frown and smile simultaneously.

Part of her was liking being with Brett, but another part of her, like a pang of hunger gnawing at her stomach, wanted Sam back here, too. So she could sit and listen to them talk and laugh and be boys, like she always had. Her husband, Brett and Logan.

Brett cleared his throat and Jamie's eyes snapped up to meet his. She had no idea whether he was waiting for her to say something, or whether he was just watching her.

"Jamie, what do you say?" he asked.

She raised her eyebrows, wishing she hadn't been daydreaming. "To what?"

"Logan's in town for the next week and he wanted to know if you're free tonight. We thought we'd go grab a few drinks, catch up."

Jamie liked that they were trying to include her, but she didn't want to be a third wheel. "You guys just hang out. You don't need to ask me along."

Brett put his hand over the phone and

leaned toward her, eyes never leaving hers. "Please come," he said, reaching for her with his other hand, fingers closing over hers. "I'll pick you up on my way and drop you at your door at the end of the night. Come out and have fun, we both want to take you out."

She looked from his eyes to his fingers over hers, wished that it was just a platonic gesture, that his skin against hers wasn't sending a shiver up and down her spine.

"Okay," she said, not needing any more convincing.

Brett grinned and pulled away, leaning back in his chair again and discussing details with Logan. She was pleased their coffees arrived at the same time as he hung up, needing something to distract her. Somehow she'd gone from hanging out with her husband's friend, to being on edge about agreeing to a night out. It was only supposed to be an evening with friends, so why was her stomach twisting like she was going on a first date?

"Sugar?"

Jamie nodded and reached for it, careful not to touch Brett's hand again.

"So Logan's back for a while, too?" she asked.

"He's still working, but he's based in Australia indefinitely."

"And you're sure he was okay about me tagging along on a boys' night?"

Brett cut the chocolate peppermint slice into two pieces and nudged one in her direction. "Since when are you not allowed to tag along on a boys' night? I don't recall Sam ever leaving you at home when we used to catch up."

"True." Brett was right, she *had* always hung out with them. But now that it was just her, she didn't want them feeling sorry for her and feeling like they had to include her.

"When was the last time you went out?" he asked.

"Can I pass on that question?" Jamie laughed and took a bite of the slice. "It's been a while."

"If another guy so much as looks at you he'll have me to deal with, so you're in safe hands."

Jamie picked at some chocolate and then took a sip of coffee, because she didn't want to make eye contact with Brett. There was only one guy she was worried about, and he was sitting directly across from her. He might trust himself, but she wasn't entirely sure that her thoughts were as pure.

CHAPTER THREE

Jamie padded barefoot into the kitchen and fed Bear. She poured herself a glass of water and leaned on the counter, slowly drinking it, concentrating on the cool liquid and how it felt as she swallowed. It was the only thing she could think of to calm her nerves, other than going for a run, and after the time she'd spent in the shower and doing her hair, she had no intention of getting sweaty.

What was she doing?

It wasn't the fact that she was going out that was making her feel guilty, because she was in desperate need of doing something fun that got her out of the house. Her problem was that she couldn't stop thinking about Brett, and it was making her feel things that she had no right to feel.

She'd dolled herself up, made more of an

effort than she had in months to look good, and it was Brett she was trying to impress. It was as if all the years of flirting had finally caught up with them, and with Sam not here, things were starting to feel awkward, fast. Or maybe not so much awkward as *exciting*.

"Brett is forbidden. Brett is my friend," she muttered, realizing that she was looking at her dog as if he were part of the conversation. "Tell me I'm crazy, Bear. I'm crazy, aren't I?"

He just stared up at her, pausing, before going back to eating his dinner.

Jamie sighed and dumped her water glass in the sink before walking back to her bedroom and looking at the clothes she'd thrown on the bed. She had her little black dress, a pair of satin pants and a sexy top, and her favorite skinny jeans. She reached for the dress and held it up, looking at her reflection in the floor-length mirror behind the door.

She wanted to wear the dress. She wanted to make Brett notice her. *She wanted to feel sexy.*

Jamie stripped down to her underwear and slipped on the dress. She was about to reach for a pair of five-inch black heels that she'd never worn before, that were just stuck in her closet, when her hand stopped moving. Everything stopped. Because just above her shoe rack, hanging on a little hook, was her husband's dog tag on its silver chain.

Jamie slowly reached for it, fingers clasping the cool metal, tracing over the tag that she'd spent so many hours staring at since he'd gone. The same tag that she'd often touched when they'd been lying together, in bed on a lazy morning....

"If anything ever happened to you, would they give me this?"

Sam frowned. "Nothing's going to happen to me, baby, but yeah. They would."

She reached for it again, turning it over and reading the inscription out aloud. "Samuel Harvey Mattheson. O positive."

"Are you going to recite all my vitals, too?"

Jamie lay her head on Sam's bare chest, still holding his tag as she shut her eyes.

"Don't ever leave me, Sam. You have to promise to come home."

He kissed the top of her head. "Baby, I'm coming home. Haven't I always told you that nothing could keep me away from you?"

"How can you be so sure?" She kissed his chest, lips against his warm skin, before moving up and kissing his mouth, trying to stop tears from falling down her cheeks and onto his face.

"If I don't, then promise me you'll wear this. I don't ever want you to forget me, Jamie...."

Jamie had sunk to the floor, tears pricking her eyes then falling in a slow, steady trickle down her cheeks and into her mouth. What was she doing? How could she even be *thinking* about Brett like she had been? What was wrong with her?

But she knew. Deep down, she knew.

There had been a spark between her and Brett for years, a spark that could have easily turned into something more if they'd met at the right time, and now he was here and she was a widow. Her feelings were only natural. But they were also wrong. Being lonely wasn't an excuse to give in to any of those feelings, not now, not ever.

Jamie reached back up for the tag and took it down, slipping it around her neck. She needed Sam close to her, wanted him close to her, and she was upset that she'd forgot-

ten the promise she'd made to him that she'd
wear it.

She also slipped back out of the dress, suddenly not wanting to make Brett notice her
like that. She reached for her skinny jeans
instead, paired them with heels and pulled
a scoop-neck tank over her head. Jamie
finished the look with a biker-style leather
jacket and hoop earrings, before going back
into the bathroom to fix her makeup. She
smoothed foundation over her tearstains, put
on some more mascara and touched up her
lip gloss, before running a hand through her
smooth hair—courtesy of her straightening
iron.

When the doorbell rang and Bear started
barking, she took one final look in the mirror and kissed Sam's dog tag.

Tonight, he was with her, looking out for
her, just like his friends were. She couldn't
stop her feelings for Brett, but she *could* stop
herself from acting on them.

"Bear, it's just Brett again."

He stopped barking as soon as she spoke,
but he stayed by her side as she opened the
door, like he had no intention of not protecting her, even if he wasn't allowed to bark.

"Hey," she said, opening the door to find him standing a few steps back from the door, hands jammed in his jean pockets.

"Hey," Brett replied, moving forward. "You look, well, *wow*."

Jamie smiled, knowing she shouldn't be so pleased that he liked the way she looked but unable to pretend otherwise. She reached for the dog tag, fingers closing around it as she looked at Brett, needing the reminder.

"You don't look so bad yourself," she heard herself say.

"Yeah? Well you look like you're going to need a bodyguard to stay safe tonight."

Jamie laughed. "Well, lucky I have two of them, huh?"

It was true—she could have worn the dress if she hadn't been feeling so guilty, because Brett and Logan would act like her overprotective big brothers if a guy so much as looked at her too long, let alone if anyone tried anything on her.

"So shall we go?" Brett asked.

"Just let me check I've locked everything, and I need to grab my purse."

She disappeared back into the kitchen and

then the living room, double-checking all the locks.

"You know Bear would maul any strangers who even tried to come in here, right?"

Jamie glanced across at Brett, knew he was watching her. He quickly looked up and met her gaze when she caught him out, but it sent a ripple of delight through her body that he *was* staring at her, no matter what she'd been telling herself as she stood in the closet.

"So not only do I have personal bodyguards escorting me tonight, you're telling me that I have one living in my house now? A big, furry, ninety-pound one?"

Brett held up her purse for her and waited for her to walk ahead of him down the hall. Her face flushed as she realized he could be checking out her butt.

"I'm saying that you're safe with Bear here, and you're definitely safe with me," he told her, his voice a note lower than it had been earlier.

Jamie glanced over her shoulder and waited for Brett to follow her out the door. Then she locked it and looped her hand through his arm. She could have so easily dropped her head to his shoulder, given him a hug, but she didn't want to blur the lines of their friendship. Once she wouldn't have thought twice about touching him like that, because before it had never meant anything, but she knew he was feeling the change between them and the spark that seemed to have ignited since he'd walked back into her life.

"Thanks for taking me out tonight," she told him, ignoring everything else and saying the one thing she needed him to hear. "I feel like I've been alone for a really long time, and it's nice to just get out of the house and have fun."

The taxi was waiting for them, and he opened the door for her to slide in before sitting beside her.

"Here's to a good night," he said, covering her knee with his hand.

But as soon as he did it, he backed off. Fast. Because the way he looked at her, the way she couldn't help but look back at him when he touched her, must have scared him as much as it damn well terrified her.

CHAPTER FOUR

"THIS FEELS WEIRD," Jamie said as they walked through the door of the bar.

Brett couldn't have agreed more. He felt like they were on a date, the two of them heading out for the evening, and it didn't help that he was thinking things he wished he wasn't about Jamie. The music was loud but not overpowering, and because it was still early it wasn't completely packed with people yet.

He looked around for Logan, desperate to see him. Once they found him, he could go get some drinks, leave the pair of them to catch up and deal with getting his head in the right space. It was bad enough that he'd spent the day before with Jamie, but seeing her again tonight was too much, too soon.

"There he is."

Jamie was leaning into him, talking into his ear over the noise and the music. He looked where she was pointing, groaning as she took hold of his hand. He got it; she was probably nervous about being out on the town without her husband, was reaching to him for support. But the way he was feeling right now, he didn't need her hand thrust into his, fingers interlaced as she walked slightly ahead of him toward Logan.

When they reached him Brett pulled his hand away and ran it through his hair instead. He needed to get it together, and fast. Logan would notice straight away if anything was going on, and he didn't want to be interrogated by anyone—especially not his best mate. Logan would be the first person to call him to task if he knew even the half of what he'd been thinking.

"Hey, Jamie." Logan jumped off the bar stool and wrapped his arms around her, giving her a big hug.

When he let go, Brett stepped forward and greeted him, grabbing hold of one of his hands and slapping him on the back at the same time. They hadn't seen each other in months.

"How are you, stranger?"

Brett shrugged. "Better now I've seen you."

They stared at one another, so much unsaid, but it only lasted a moment. Logan knew what had happened, would be the only person in Brett's life who would ever come close to understanding what he'd experienced, although even he couldn't imagine how disturbing it had been, how violent. They hadn't seen each other in a long while, had a lot of catching up to do.

Brett shook off his thoughts. "What are we drinking? My shout."

"Start with a beer or straight to bourbon?" Logan asked.

Jamie laughed, and Brett angled his body to better include her. He'd been so wound up in seeing Logan again that he'd almost forgotten about her. Brett touched his palm to her back, moving her forward between them and taking a step back to make room for her.

"I think we'll start with beer. How about you?"

Jamie smiled. "Um, maybe a cocktail for me."

Logan raised his eyebrows and Brett

laughed. "So maybe we'll start with bourbon then, if you're hitting the strong stuff straight away."

Jamie leaned over the counter to reach for a menu. "It's been a *looong* time since I've been out. Can't you tell? The only cocktail I can think of is a Cosmopolitan from *Sex and the City*, but there must be something else...."

"Long Island iced teas," Logan announced. "Three of them."

Jamie pushed her shoulders up, shrugging, an innocent expression on her face. Brett needed to warn her.

"They're kind of potent," he said.

Her smile was sweet enough to make him feel dirty for admiring her cleavage when she leaned forward.

"Lucky I have you two to look after me then, huh?" She put an arm around each of them, her smile infectious. "I need a night of just having fun, so order away, boys. I'm in."

Brett did as he was told and watched her walk off with Logan, looking for a quieter, more comfortable place to sit. They all had a lot to talk about, or maybe they didn't. Maybe tonight was about letting Jamie have fun without feeling guilty, just being there for her and making sure she had a good time and got home safely at the end of the evening.

He just had to remind himself that he would have plenty to be guilty about if he ever let himself give in to the way he was feeling about her. Brett paid for the drinks and stuffed his wallet back in his pocket, before carrying their drinks to the table. He could see Jamie leaning toward Logan, talking, touching his shoulder as they discussed something that had her smiling. Logan was rock-solid, the perfect guy to be spending time with Jamie, because he would honor his word and never do anything that would jeopardize their friendship or the one he'd had with Sam. Trouble was, it wasn't Logan who was spending time with Jamie, because he was still working.

"Drink up," he announced, placing the tall glasses on the table and sitting down beside Jamie.

The way she looked at him took him by surprise, made him hope that Logan hadn't noticed it, but maybe he was just being over-sensitive.

"To Sam," Logan said, holding up his drink. "A good soldier, a damn good friend and husband to the sweetest woman I've ever met."

Brett glanced at Jamie, saw her eyes were damp. He held up his own glass. "Cheers to that."

They all took a sip, but Jamie was spluttering as soon as she'd swallowed her first mouthful.

"Are you guys trying to kill me? This stuff is like poison."

Brett laughed. "It gets better. Just keep drinking."

"Has Brett shown you his new tattoo?" Logan asked.

Jamie shook her head, looking at him. "Nope." She took another sip and grimaced again.

"Brett had his done as soon as he was out of recovery, and I got mine when I touched down in Australia."

"You have new matching ones?" she asked. "Can I see?"

Logan pushed his T-shirt up, rolling his arm around to show the words marked in black ink, curling letters over four short rows.

"'Fight a battle for a cause that's worth the victory. Fight a war that's worth dying for. Remain brave in death. Honor those you love.'" Jamie stared at Logan's arm as she finished reading the words.

Brett knew she was fighting emotion, because her voice had become low and husky, a deeper tone than he'd ever heard from her. He responded by rolling up his shirt until he could show her his matching ink, only just able to push the fabric high enough for her to see it.

Jamie turned to inspect his properly, trailing her fingers across each word as if she were writing them, committing them to memory. Her touch was light, and when her hand dropped to land on his thigh, it almost made him lose the drink he'd just reached for.

"You did these for Sam, didn't you?" she asked.

Brett nodded when she looked at him, and Logan did the same.

"Well, they're beautiful," she said, dabbing her eyes with the back of her fingers. "Maybe I should get one, too?"

"No," Brett said, faster than he'd meant to.

"I don't think so," Logan chimed in, almost as quickly.

Jamie raised an eyebrow, looking puzzled. "Because I'm a girl? They're not exactly military tattoos, are they?"

Brett looked to Logan for help but didn't receive any. He cleared his throat, not wanting to dig himself a hole that he couldn't claw his way out of, but not having any intention of letting her ink herself.

"Your skin is beautiful and you don't need any ink, Jamie. Don't go rushing into anything."

"Just keep wearing that tag," Logan added. "It's what he would have wanted."

She laughed and took a hearty sip of her drink, before slowly downing the rest of it.

"Bottoms up, boys," she announced, grinning at them over the top of her glass.

Brett and Logan exchanged looks before shrugging and following her lead.

"My round this time. Another?" Jamie asked.

They both said yes and watched her walk away, like two bodyguards ready to pounce on anyone who so much as bumped into her.

"'Your skin is so beautiful'?" Logan mimicked, punching him in the arm. "Seriously, couldn't you have come up with anything better than that?"

Brett glared at him. "It wasn't like you were stepping in to help me out."

"Yeah, I was too busy watching you swooning over her. You know she's out of bounds, right? Because I'll…"

Brett gave him a playful shove, trying to laugh the comment off. "You don't have to tell me, I know."

"I miss him, Brett. I seriously miss him."

Brett leaned back in his seat, watching Jamie at the bar as she leaned toward the bartender to place her order. He couldn't believe he hadn't noticed the dog tag she was wearing around her neck, but then he'd been trying his hardest not to look at her chest, and the way the tag was being swallowed by her breasts… Brett cleared his throat. That wasn't something he needed to think about right now. Sam had been like his surrogate brother, and he would never disrespect anyone he considered family.

"I can't stop thinking about that day. It's screwed up, Logan. The things I saw, what happened, I just wish I could forget it all, for good."

Brett shut his eyes, blocked the memories out, doing what he always did. Because forcing them away was a damn sight easier than dealing with them, and he didn't want to go there, not now.

"I'm going to go help her carry the drinks back," he announced, needing to move.

Before Logan guessed that he also couldn't stop thinking about Jamie, in all the wrong ways.

Jamie leaned back into Brett, eyes shut, the room starting to spin. She'd had three cocktails, but she wasn't exactly used to drinking and it felt like three too many.

"I don't feel so good."

Brett's arm was suddenly looped around her shoulders, holding her closer to his body. She opened her eyes to look at Logan, but he was starting to blur.

"I think someone needs something to eat," Logan said.

"And water," she mumbled.

Logan jumped up and gave her what she

guessed was a salute. "Glass of water and greasy fries coming up."

She tucked back tighter into Brett, starting to feel sleepy.

"Thanks for looking after me."

His chuckle made his chest vibrate beneath her ear.

"They were pretty potent," he told her, his hold on her shoulders loosening as he bent forward to retrieve his drink. "We shouldn't have let you have more than two."

Jamie groaned. "You're going to take me home, right?" She didn't want to have to flag a taxi on her own in the dark, not to mention go home to an empty house. Most nights, she tried to remind herself why she was okay alone, but tonight her brain just wasn't cooperating.

"We weren't exactly going to get you drunk then let you find your own way home."

Jamie shut her eyes again, wishing she had only had two drinks. They'd been having so much fun, and she hadn't been out in so long.

"Brett, can you stay with me tonight?" she asked.

Jamie thought she felt his body stiffen, but maybe she was imagining it.

"Ah, I'm not sure," he said. "I'll see you home, though."

Jamie shook her head and turned, hand on Brett's shoulder as she stared up at him. "Please? I just don't want to be alone tonight."

He looked down at her and she couldn't read his face. Having her eyes shut and sitting still for a few minutes had made the spinning stop, but she was still feeling less than average.

"If you still want me to stay when we get to your place, then I will," he finally said. "Just don't go saying anything to Logan because he'll go off and get the wrong idea and I don't need him getting all crazy protective over you."

She smiled up at him, leaning in to kiss his cheek. It was warm and slightly stubbled, but where she kissed him was soft enough to make her want to keep her lips there. Jamie had only meant it as an innocent thank-you, but she could have easily moved slightly to the left, kissed his lips instead. She was staring at them, eyes unable to leave his mouth, even as his hand came up between them and gently pushed her back into her seat.

"Let's not do anything we'd regret sober, okay?"

Brett's voice was soft, but the hungry eyes staring back at her were telling a different story entirely.

"Who's hungry?"

Logan had returned with the bar food, which looked perfect and greasy.

"Me, please," she responded, her thigh pressed to Brett's as she leaned forward. She was telling herself she needed it there to anchor her in place, keep her steady, but she knew better.

She was drunk and coming on to her husband's friend. It was a hundred shades of wrong, but it felt every shade of right. Jamie reached for a fry and dunked it in ketchup, closing her eyes with delight at the salty, greasy taste.

"These are *sooo* good," she murmured.

Logan laughed. "Drunk as a skunk."

She didn't care what they said. Tonight had been better than good, it had been amazing. For the first time in forever, she felt like herself again, and it had been a long time coming.

Because for a while there, she'd wondered if she'd lost that Jamie forever.

Jamie held on to Brett's arm as she stepped out of the taxi, and she didn't let it go as they walked to her front door. He hadn't said anything about staying or not staying, and even though she'd sobered up a heap, she still didn't want to be alone. Nights like tonight brought everything crashing back to her, even though it had been over a decade ago.

It had been pitch-black outside, and she'd been tucked under a blanket, alone, waiting for her mom to come home. She knew she'd be drunk, but she wanted to wait for her to come back. When the door had opened, she'd stayed still, not made a sound, knowing her mom would just make her way upstairs and collapse on her bed.

Only it hadn't been her mom. She'd hidden, terrified, as two men in balaclavas had burgled their house, never making a noise so they wouldn't know anyone was home. Tears had choked in her throat, but she'd stayed silent, wishing that her dad had made it back. Knowing that if he'd been alive, her mom would still be holding it together, that she would have been safe.

"So here we are," Brett said when they reached the door, jolting her from her thoughts.

She fumbled in her bag for her keys and called out to Bear as his loud bark boomed through the door. Letting her memories take hold was not something she usually let happen, not that easily.

"Just me," she told her dog, "it's only me."

His barking stopped and she turned the key. Brett leaned past her and pushed the door, standing his ground as she dropped to give the dog a cuddle and then usher him back inside.

"Are you going to be okay on your own?" he asked, looking uncomfortable, hands jammed in his pockets.

Jamie wasn't going to lie to him, especially not now. "I've never been okay on my own," she admitted. "Every time Sam went away, I'd pretend to be all brave because

I didn't want him worrying about me, but when he was on tour I hardly ever went out unless I could be back before dark. I was just too nervous coming home to an empty house."

His expression changed, his face sad. "Is it better with Bear here?"

She nodded. "Yeah, a little."

"You still want me to stay tonight, don't you?"

Jamie nodded again. Relief took away the tightness in her shoulders as she realized she was actually going to have someone in the house. That Brett, one of the people she trusted most in the world, was going to be sleeping under her roof, protecting her, letting her have a good night's sleep without her worrying about every creak or rustle outside the window. Without her thinking someone might find their way into her home.

Brett smiled when she stepped back, and he walked into the house and locked the door behind him.

"I'll just bunk on the sofa," he said, following her into the kitchen.

"I can make up the spare bed," she told

him, flicking on a light and fumbling in the pantry for coffee. "I don't want you being uncomfortable."

"Hey," Brett said, coming up behind her and taking the coffee. "You go sit down, I'll make us both a cup. I'm sure your head could do without all the movement, might help the pounding stop."

His hand over hers made her freeze, and she resisted the urge to push back into him, to rock her body back into his like she was so desperate to do. She craved his touch like a desperate woman who'd never had the pleasure of a man before.

"Go sit on the sofa," he ordered, voice low.

Jamie reluctantly did as she was told, listening to Brett as he moved around the kitchen. She flopped onto the big sofa, tucked up against a cushion, eyes back on him as he stirred two cups and then carried them over. He placed them down and went to sit on the armchair.

"It's way more comfy over here," she told him.

He hesitated before coming over to sit beside her. Jamie tucked her feet up and changed position, her body against Brett's instead of the oversized cushion. Now she had an oversized, warm, muscled man to lean into.

"Thanks for tonight," she told him.

"My pleasure," he responded, staying still but looking down at her.

Jamie knew she was still a little drunk, that she needed to just sleep it off and not do anything stupid, but ever since she'd kissed Brett at the bar, on the cheek, she'd thought of nothing other than his lips; his full, kissable lips.

Before she knew what she was doing, she reached up to touch his face, tracing her fingers over his mouth before leaning on him and putting her lips there. It was a sweet kiss, a warm kiss, a kiss that made her skin tingle. And it wasn't easy to pull back from. Brett didn't resist, didn't push her away, but he didn't move closer, either. He just moved his lips enough for her to know that he was kissing her back, that he wanted it, too. Or at least that's what she wanted to think.

He didn't say anything when she pulled away, and neither did she. Brett reached for a cushion, put it at the end of the sofa and leaned back into it, letting her fall down against him. She put her head against his chest, tucked up beside him, like a cat purring into his hold as he put his arm around her.

She should have gone and found a blanket to keep them warm, but she didn't want to move and Brett was warm and snuggly even without anything covering them. Instead she shut her eyes and let sleep catch her and wrap her in its equally warm embrace. She couldn't have fought it if she tried, and Jamie had a feeling that for once she might actually sleep through the entire night without waking, terrified, like she usually did.

Brett stared down at Jamie. She was asleep, he could hear the change in her breathing, but it didn't make him even close to being sleepy himself.

Jamie, Sam's wife, had just kissed him. And he'd done nothing to stop it and everything to encourage it.

Granted, he'd had a lot to drink, but not enough to make him drunk or to make him forget that she was forbidden. Even Logan had reminded him, just in case he'd managed to forget himself, that she was the one woman he wasn't supposed to think about, *like that.* And yet she'd come on to him and he'd willingly accepted her advances.

But then he'd known he was a goner tonight from the moment she'd traced her fingers down his inner arm, along the words of his tattoo, and he'd known he was incapable of doing the right thing when she'd kissed his cheek in the bar. The heat of her breath against his skin, her warm lips, the look in her eyes…like she wanted him, trusted him and needed him, all rolled into one stare. Into one gentle touch that he found one hundred percent irresistible.

Brett groaned, but there was no getting away from her, not now that she was clutching his shirt between her fingers and her head was tucked against his chest like it was her own personal pillow to snuggle up into.

The light in the kitchen was still on, but unless he could teach the dog how to turn it off, he was just going to have to shut his eyes and do his best to ignore it.

He caught sight of Bear watching him, head between his paws, eyebrows raised.

"Don't look at me like that," Brett told him, scowling.

He didn't need a damn dog to make him feel even more guilty than he already felt.

"And don't you be forgetting that I saved your life," he muttered, before shutting his eyes.

The truth was that Bear had saved all of them that day. He'd stopped after Sam had sent him out, body dead-still, tail quivering, head cocked to the side. It had been Bear who'd alerted them to the bomb—only trouble was that it wasn't a standard improvised explosive device. This IED had been remote-detonated, most likely from a local hiding where they hadn't been able to find him. Someone watching, in wait, to explode an entire 4x4 full of SAS soldiers, wanting to blow them all into pieces.

Sam and Brett's dog had been the casualties that day, so maybe he should be showing Bear some respect and thanking *him* for saving his life.

He shut his eyes, knowing sleep wouldn't come easily, because it never did these days. If he managed to fall asleep, he'd wake up in a sweat and twisted in his sheets, mind full of the darkness of that day he was trying so hard to forget. And then he'd lie awake, scared of shutting his eyes again because of the memories that flashed like scenes from a movie beneath his eyelids.

CHAPTER FIVE

WHEN BRETT WOKE up, the pain in his leg and back hit him straight away. He was all crooked from lying flat, and when he tried to move, he realized he couldn't. Because the woman he'd just been having an erotic dream about was still attached to his chest, her long hair splayed out across him, arm slung down low, cheek to his heart.

He shut his eyes again, remembering how uncomfortable it had been carrying a hundred-and-fifty-pound pack when he was on patrol with the SAS. At least Jamie was warm and... He swallowed away that particular thought. Now he just had to hope that she didn't wake up for a little bit longer, so she didn't have to wonder if it was a gun or if he was just pleased to see her when she realized where her hand was resting.

But…he'd slept. He'd dreamed about Jamie. And he wasn't wet with sweat. Which meant that last night was the first night he'd actually slept through, without nightmares, since *that day*.

When Brett opened his eyes again, Bear was staring back at him, his nose right beside his face, as if he'd just been waiting for them to wake up.

"Hey, buddy," he whispered, receiving a giant lick in reply.

Jamie groaned then and wriggled closer against him, her arm flinging across his chest. He kept one hand on her to keep her in place, not wanting her to fall off the sofa if she stretched the other way. Another low groan told him she perhaps wasn't a morning person, or that her head was starting to thump.

"Want some pain meds?" he asked, keeping his voice low.

She went still, then put her palm flat on his chest and pushed up. Her hair was all messy, curlier than he'd ever seen it, and her eyes were smudged. She looked lazy and sexy all rolled into one.

"I slept on you."

He chuckled. "We still have our clothes on, so don't worry."

She didn't smile, so he was guessing his joke wasn't in the best taste, but she did flop back down on top of him, face buried in his chest again.

"My head kind of hurts," she muttered. "And don't even try to tell me I don't look like crap, because I know I do."

He laughed. "You actually look pretty good."

Funny how he could go from freaking out to joking with her in two seconds flat, and he wasn't lying, either.

"Warmed-up crap," she muttered. "That's even worse than straight crap, right?"

Brett pushed her gently off him and stretched, being careful to flex his leg before standing up. He'd missed a few physical therapy sessions since he'd been back, and the last thing he needed was to do damage to his just-recovered leg because he was too lazy to stretch.

"I'm going to get you a glass of water and something for your head. Where do you keep the meds?"

"In the bathroom," she mumbled.

Brett stood and crossed the room. If he were going to pretend like he was here just to protect her, to look after her, he may as well do something to actually be helpful.

Jamie excused herself, went up to her bathroom and took a long shower. She just stood there under the burning hot water, letting it pour down her face and hair. Her head had stopped pounding, thanks to the tablets she'd just swallowed, but she was still feeling a lot less perky than she usually did.

She forced herself to step out of the shower and wrapped a massive towel around her small frame, using a different one to dry her long hair. After what had happened last night she was in no hurry to rush back downstairs to Brett, not after she'd gone ahead and kissed him. Her only hope was that maybe he thought she'd been too drunk to remember it. *She wished.*

Jamie rubbed moisturizer onto her body, then applied some makeup, smoothing on some foundation, then mascara, blush and lip gloss. She didn't want to look like she'd gone to too much effort, but then she didn't want him to see her looking hungover with no makeup on, either.

She heard a noise behind her and jumped, but it was only Bear. The last thing she needed was Brett walking in on her naked, wearing only a dog tag around her neck. The dog tag that was supposed to remind her, no matter what, that a certain friend of her husband's was out of bounds.

"Hey, buddy." Bear was staring at her with his head cocked to the side, and she was pleased to think about something other than her behavior the night previous. "You hungry?"

Her stomach growled in response to her own question, so she left her hair pinned up wet and signaled for her dog to follow her. She wasn't used to drinking, and she sure as hell wasn't used to dealing with a hangover.

Jamie removed the dog tag and slung it back on the hook by her shoes, feeling like a traitor for wearing it after the way she'd behaved with Brett the night before, and pulled on jeans and a T-shirt. Then she walked down the hall to find Brett with the morning paper, sprawled out over the kitchen counter as he ate a piece of toast.

"Hey," she said as she went straight for the coffee.

He looked up and held his toast in his mouth as he shuffled the paper so it took up less space.

"How you feeling now?" he asked with a grin.

Jamie groaned. "Please don't remind me about last night." She poured herself a large cup of coffee, stirred in two sugars and took a gulp. It was piping hot and burned her tongue but she didn't care.

She scooped a cup of Bear's special dog biscuits into his bowl, aware that he'd been patiently waiting at her feet since they'd arrived in the kitchen, then went back to nursing her coffee.

"I'm feeling a bit responsible for plying you with those drinks," he said, finishing his toast. "Maybe we should have gone with beer, or just let you a have a few girly cocktails instead of the most potent blend on the menu."

Jamie held up her hand. "I'll take full responsibility for drinking them, so long as you don't ever mention the words *Long Island iced tea* to me *ever* again."

Brett laughed and held up his coffee cup. "Deal," he agreed. "You want me to make you anything for brekkie while you nurse your head?"

She groaned again, sipping more coffee. "I'll just have toast, thanks. Cold toast with jam, something easy on my poor stomach."

The way Brett was watching her told her he was thinking about something, waiting to ask her something. Please don't bring up the kiss. The last thing she needed right now was to deal with that particular conversation, especially before she'd eaten anything and had time to process it.

"Jamie, I don't know if you remember, but when we were at the bar, and then when we came back here last night…"

She gulped when he paused, and then he said, "You mentioned that you never told Sam how scared you were coming home to an empty house in the dark."

Phew. She could deal with this conversation if she had to. It might have been difficult to talk about, admitting to that, but given what the alternative topic could have been, she was relieved.

"My dad was a soldier, and he died on deployment, too." Jamie kept her gaze trained on her coffee, not wanting to look at Brett. "When he died, my mom went on a bender that lasted a few years, and I was home alone when we were burgled. I hid until they left, but I guess I've never really gotten over that fear of it happening again. Which is why I'm obsessed with locking doors and being inside before sundown, and my security alarm was always on before Bear came back to live here."

Brett was still staring at her, concern written all over his face. "So I'm guessing you told Sam about what happened, but you never told him how much it still scared you. Because you always knew that he'd be going away and leaving you alone. That there was nothing he could do to change that."

Jamie nodded.

"I can't believe he was away for months at a time, and you had to be a prisoner inside your own house every night. You should have told us."

She sighed and moved closer to him, staying on the other side of the kitchen counter and leaning forward. "I just always had that fear of going to sleep and not knowing if someone could have gotten into the house while I was out. There's nothing Sam could have done for me, except worry like crazy from the other side of the world, and that wouldn't have been good for either of us."

"But you're sleeping okay now?"

She shook her head, not wanting to tell the truth but wanting to lie to Brett even less. "Last night was the first time since before Sam deployed that I've slept through without waking. I've been better with Bear here this last month, so I'm not complaining, but being alone isn't something I've ever been good at. I freak out at every sound and then can't fall asleep again."

Brett stared into his coffee cup, which she was sure must have been empty by now. "Did you sleep better because I was here with you, or because of the alcohol?"

Jamie grinned at him. "Last night might well have been a combination of both, but I have no intentions of turning into an alcoholic just to sleep through the night. Plus I have no plans of turning into my mom."

He smiled, but he wasn't laughing at her joke. "Let me stay for a few days, let you catch up on some sleep while I'm here."

His voice was lower than usual, an octave deeper. She shook her head. "You don't have to do that. I'll be fine."

She might have been telling him no, but inside she was screaming out for him to stay. Having Brett here would make her feel safe, let her relax and just sleep solidly for a few nights at least, but she didn't expect him to do that.

And her intentions weren't pure, either. Because ever since she'd starting thinking about Brett in a certain way last night, re-membering how soft his lips had been, how sensual it had been pressed against his body, she'd thought of nothing other than having him here. Keeping him close. Wondering if something could happen between them, and whether he wanted it as much as she did, even if she did know it was wrong.

She took a deep breath. "I don't want you feeling sorry for me."

That made him smile. "I most definitely don't feel sorry for you," he said. "And it's no big deal. If you want me to stay, just say so. Besides, sleeping isn't exactly easy for me these days, and I slept through the night last night, too."

"If I'm honest, Brett, having you here for a few days sounds idyllic." She wanted to stay strong, but she also wanted a man in her house again. Wanted the company of someone she could actually talk to, who wasn't afraid of the truth. Of what had happened to her husband. Because she had no one else to talk to, and no one else to turn to. She'd lost her dad and then her husband to war, and she was tired of being alone. "But only if you're sure."

She listened to Brett's big intake of breath, watched the way his body stiffened then softened back to normal again. When they weren't serving, Sam's two best friends had been as much a part of her life as her husband had, and she missed having them all around. It was like she'd lost all three of them at once.

"Then I'll stay. As long as you need me here, I'll stay."

She dropped her head to his shoulder. "He would have liked you being here, you know that, right?"

Brett shrugged, but she could tell he was finding this as awkward as she was. "You know, he made me promise to look out for you if anything ever happened to him. I just never figured that we'd actually be in that position."

Jamie smiled. "I'll never forget what you've done for me, Brett."

Brett was her friend. Nothing more. She just had to keep reminding herself of that, because falling in love with her husband's best buddy? Not something that could happen. Not now, not ever.

Brett could have been the man of her dreams—*once*. But now wasn't the time to look back. Now was about the future. The one she had to build without her husband by her side. No matter how much she was thinking about *that* kiss.

"Well, if you're staying you're definitely not sleeping on the sofa."

He shrugged. "Whatever's easy for you. I don't want to be any trouble."

Jamie poured herself another cup of coffee and gestured for him to pass his cup over for more. "You never did say how long you were back for? What your plans were?"

Brett took the now full cup from her and looked at her over the counter. "I'm kind of done with the army."

She felt her eyebrows shoot up. "What do you mean by *kind of?*"

"I mean that I've served my time and now I'm retired. Honorable discharge."

"Wow." Jamie hadn't even considered that he might have left the army, that he was done with a role he'd been in for so many years. "Did it have something to do with what happened?" She didn't want to bring it up again, but she also wanted to know.

The relief that hit her body, knowing that there was no chance she could lose Brett, too, was like a physical weight lifting from her shoulders. The last thing she'd need was to worry herself silly the next time both Brett and Logan were deployed. She'd lost too many men in her life to deal with the possibility of losing another.

"I was burned pretty bad on my leg and back, so my injuries were enough to put me out of action for a while, but to be honest I think I've given enough to the cause. I don't think I could have gone back on deployment again after what happened, after what I went through. It's changed how I'd react to a situation."

"So you'll be staying with the army, though?" she asked. "Doing something with dogs still?"

Brett shrugged. "I need to spend some time figuring my life out, what I want to do, where I want to be." He took a sip of coffee, a thoughtful look on his face as he stared out the window. "Right now I can't imagine a life that doesn't involve working with a dog all day, being deployed or training for the next task-force operation. So I just need some time to process everything."

"Can you take your time deciding?"

He nodded. "Yeah, I can. I need to focus on recovering fully, then I can figure out what I'm going to do long-term. Start over, I guess."

And he was going to be doing a lot of that figuring out here, if she had anything to do with where he would be spending his time while he was in Sydney.

"So when you say you hurt your leg and back badly..." she began, not wanting to push him but desperate to know.

"It means I should be doing physio stretches and exercises every day," Brett confessed, "starting this morning."

"Well, it just so happens that I have a heap

of work to do, so how about you do what you need to do and I'll sit in my office and try to get this book finished."

Brett grinned. "Deal."

Brett smiled at the physical therapist through the computer screen. It wasn't ideal, but he'd been through rehabilitation and all the hard grunt as far as his leg was concerned, and now it was just a matter of gaining the muscle strength that he'd lost and getting his body back to full capacity.

"So you're not pushing yourself too hard yet?"

He laughed. "Not doing enough is more the problem."

"Well, best I can advise you is to do your stretches daily, and start doing some light jogging if you're up to it. Then you can slowly get back to the point where any type of exercise will be okay."

He gave her a salute. "Yes, ma'am."

She grinned. "Pleased to see you have your spark back. Obviously someone's been looking after you now that you're back home."

Brett glanced up, looked at Jamie working through the open window of her office. "I'm just pleased to be back," he told her.

"Okay, show me your leg stretches, both sides, and then you can get back to doing whatever it is that's making you smile."

He was pleased he'd decided to use video messaging to contact her, because otherwise another day would have passed without him doing the exercises. Before he'd come to see Jamie, he hadn't missed a day, but she'd been more than a little distracting. The fact that she was working and could look out at him wasn't exactly helping his powers of concentration, but he needed to block her out.

How many times had he had to just focus and get on with a task for work? Ignoring one woman shouldn't have been a struggle, but it was.

Brett ran through the exercises, lifting both legs separately, tightening and releasing and then jumping up and down as he'd been shown to do.

"What do you think?" he asked, slightly out of breath once he'd finished the series of reps.

The physical therapist nodded. "Good work. Just keep it up and extend yourself a little bit more every day. You'll get a feel for how hard you can push your body."

They said goodbye and he stood up, slowly stretching before doing some fast sprints back and forth across the lawn. His leg twinged when he stopped too quickly, but he kept it up, taking care not to strain anything. Bear was watching him from the edge of the grass like he was crazy to be using so much energy in the heat, and he had a feeling Jamie might be watching him, too. He didn't indulge himself in looking in her direction, not yet. Because staying focused was already proving to be a task he wasn't excelling at.

When he finished he dropped to the ground to do two sets of crunches, then press-ups, before shutting his eyes and just lying in the sun. Maybe he was getting old, or maybe his body had just been through a more serious trauma than he was letting himself admit. But he was definitely ready for a shower, or a swim in a cool pool would have been even better.

"You look exhausted."

Brett opened his eyes and stared up at

Jamie. He rolled to his side and pulled up to a sitting position.

"I thought you were chained to your desk for the rest of the day?" he asked.

She sighed. "Watching you out here wasn't helping to keep me stuck in there."

"If you'd rather I went…"

"No," she replied, holding out a towel and a bottle of water before he could continue. "What I want is to forget about work and just enjoy the day."

He wiped his face and neck with the towel, before twisting the top off the water and guzzling it down.

"When's your deadline?" he asked as she flopped down to sit on the grass with him.

"End of the week," she said, as Bear came over and leaned against her, looking for attention. "I'll make it, I just can't concentrate today. Or at all, lately, if I'm completely honest. My brain just doesn't want to switch into the right gear."

Brett watched as she tried to push the dog away, laughing as he leaned on her and wouldn't give up. In the end she gave up and Bear laid upside down beside her for a belly scratch.

"For someone who keeps saying she doesn't know a lot about dogs, you're sure developing a good friendship with this one." Bear had his eyes closed now, in heaven at all the attention he was receiving.

"It's not that I don't love him, because I do," Jamie said, smiling with her eyes as she stared at him. "I just haven't ever had a dog before, and I wasn't confident with telling him what to do. Or what to expect from him."

"Love is a pretty good start," Brett said, wishing he'd chosen his words better as soon as they came out of his mouth.

"Yeah? Well I've never found it hard to love, so maybe we'll be okay after all."

Brett stayed silent, wasn't sure what to say. Just because he was thinking about last night, wishing that he hadn't been so damn honorable and pushed her away when she'd kissed him, didn't mean he needed to bring it up. The only consolation was that she didn't have anything to regret now that she was sober, because if he'd let things go too far she might not have the same smile on her face that she did right now.

"As much as I'd like to enjoy the day with

you, I think you need to get some more work done."

She groaned. "Have you been secretly talking to my editor?"

Brett grinned. "No, but you don't need this deadline hanging over your head, and you'll feel so much better for doing at least some of it today."

"You're right, I'm just procrastinating."

Brett sat up properly and stretched his legs out in front of him. "I'll make you a deal."

She raised her eyebrows. "Let me hear it."

"I'm going to head out, run a few errands and pick up some groceries. We can cook something nice for dinner, and you can forget all about your deadline, once you've worked for a few hours."

"Promise me we can have chocolate for dessert, and you have yourself a deal."

Brett held out his hand, smiling when her palm slipped into his. He was on dangerous territory, and he was starting to enjoy it.

CHAPTER SIX

It HAD BEEN a long time since Brett had shopped for groceries and arrived home to cook dinner. He kicked the door shut with the heel of his boot and carried the bags through the house, before putting them on the ground and calling out to Jamie.

"I'm back," he called, wandering down the hall toward her office.

"Oh, hey," she said back.

He walked a couple of steps backward, looking into the bedroom he'd just passed. Jamie was tucking sheets into the bed, hair pulled up into a ponytail, wearing cutoff denim shorts and a tight tank top.

He could have done without seeing Jamie looking like that, making a bed that was presumably for him. Thank God it was down the hall from her room.

"I just wanted to let you know I was back."

She smiled and threw the duvet on the bed, followed by a couple of pillows that had been sitting on the ground.

"You were secretly checking up on me, weren't you?"

Her smile was infectious, no matter how much he wished he could distance himself from her. In the car, he'd reminded himself how he needed to behave, how he needed to think about her, but no amount of good intentions could help him when he was faced with Jamie in the flesh.

She didn't seem to notice that he hadn't replied and breezed past him, her shoulder skimming his bicep as she headed down the hall.

"Before you ask, I worked solidly almost the entire time you were gone, so I don't have anything to feel guilty about."

Brett froze before he could follow her, had only managed to turn before his feet refused to move. Because staring at him, eyes on his, was Sam. Sam's smiling photo was hanging in the hall, straight outside the bedroom, and he hadn't even noticed it when he'd walked past looking for Jamie. *For Sam's wife.*

"Brett?"

He shook his head, mouthed *sorry* to his friend, the friend he was so close to betraying, and followed Jamie to the kitchen.

"Are you okay?"

Brett forced himself to snap out of whatever the hell it was he'd sunk into. She'd been Sam's wife for years, he had known that this morning and he'd known it the night before, and yet he was the one who'd suggested he stay, who'd decided to go grocery shopping for dinner. It wasn't Jamie's fault that he was flipping out over something that was every bit his fault, so he needed to pull himself together.

"Sorry, yeah, I wasn't sure what you'd like."

"Mmmm, what are we making?"

He watched as she started to pull things out of the bags. "It's the only thing I can make that doesn't involve packets of sauce or frozen food."

Brett never took his eyes off her as she laughed and pulled out a bag of tomatoes.

"Pasta?"

He nodded. "My mom was a great cook,

and it's the only thing I ever learned from her."

Jamie's face lost the rosy glow he'd been enjoying watching, her eyebrows dragging together as she frowned.

"You were only young when you lost your parents, weren't you?"

Her voice was tender and it made him want to walk straight around the kitchen and hold her, to engulf her slender body in his arms and just feel what it was like to have her pressed to him. This woman who was driving him crazy—who'd *driven* him crazy for years—was driving him wild now.

Brett cleared his throat, well past the pain of what he'd endured as a teenager, but still not a fan of dredging up the past.

"I was eighteen, and they both died in a head-on collision," he said, wishing he'd just shut his mouth and not said anything. Talking about what had happened back then was almost as bad about talking about what had happened to Sam. "I was at a party, drunk, and I phoned them to come and pick me up. Turns out they both got in the car that night, and if it hadn't been for me, they would have still been at home."

Jamie was staring at him, palms on the counter. "I can't imagine what that was like for you, Brett, but you can't honestly blame yourself."

"Actually, you're the one person who probably can understand," he said. So many people had acted like they knew what he was going through, but Jamie had only just emerged from that place of loss herself. "It's no different to you losing Sam, it's just at a different stage in your life. The only thing that isn't the same is that you had nothing to do with him dying. Me? I'll never forgive myself for making the call that took them away from me and changed my life forever."

"Brett, you were eighteen years old. Teenagers are supposed to call their parents in the middle of the night when they need them."

Brett shrugged. "Nothing anyone says to me will ever make me believe that I wasn't responsible." He stared at her, watching her mouth as it turned down into a frown. "The only thing that saved me back then was the army. I was surrounded by guys like Sam every day, and they become my surrogate family. They still are, I guess."

"So in other words you found a way to forget about what had happened."

"I'm the first to admit that I ran away from that life, but at the age I was, I didn't really have any other choice. Well, not any choice that would have been good for me."

And this was why he needed to respect Sam, even in death. He'd been family to Brett, just like the rest of his unit had been, and the last thing he needed was more guilt to carry around.

He listened to Jamie sigh before she returned to taking the groceries from the bags. "I'd run away in a heartbeat, Brett, so don't think I'd ever judge you for turning your back on the life you had taken away from you. You were brave to start over, especially in the army."

Brett should have stood his ground, just stayed still on the other side of the kitchen, but he ignored his better judgment and joined her.

"What do you want to run away from?" he asked, voice low.

"From everything about this life, from the memories, just to start over and pretend like this was all a bad dream. That I didn't choose to marry a soldier, knowing that there was a chance he'd die like my father did. I still can't believe that I lost both of them like that."

He wished he could offer it to her, wished he was brave enough to just tell her that he'd run away with her if it meant they could both forget and start over.

"I can't help you run away, Jamie, but I can help you heal."

She smiled across at him, nudged him with her shoulder. He should have resisted, but instead he slung his arm around her and pulled her in for a hug, closing his eyes when she dropped her head to his shoulder and wrapped her arm around his waist.

"I think you've already helped me," she told him, her voice laced with a softness that made him wish he wasn't thinking what he was thinking. That he was just a friend wanting to help another friend with no hidden agenda.

"What do you say I teach you how to cook Mama's tomato pasta sauce?"

She loosened her hold on him until her arm fell away, and he made himself let go of her, too.

"Was your mom Italian?"

He grinned, glanced at her before taking the tomatoes from the packet. "Sure was. And she'd kill me for buying nonorganic produce."

"Ah, well that explains the dark good looks, huh?"

Jamie was laughing and he raised an eyebrow back at her, which only made her laugh more.

"You would have liked her," he said. "And I know she'd have been impressed that I at least remembered one of her dishes."

"I have no doubt that I'd have loved the woman who raised you," she said. "Even if you did lose her young, she sure did a good job."

He looked away when Jamie leaned down to pull out the chopping board, not needing to see the way her shorts showed way too much skin when she bent forward.

"What else do you need?"

Brett reached past her for a knife from the wooden block on the counter, pleased that they were finished with their awkward conversation. He didn't mind opening up to Jamie, but going back into the past was never easy. Not for him. "You can either chop tomatoes or onions?"

"I'll do the onions," she said.

Brett went to question her, to be the gentleman and offer to do the crap job, until she reached for her sunglasses and put them on.

"Ah, smart girl."

She laughed. "Years of experience chopping these suckers. I always keep an old pair handy."

"You know this isn't going to be a quick meal, right?" he said, chopping the tomatoes into even pieces. "It needs to cook for an hour, maybe longer."

"Did you buy wine?" she asked.

"Yes, ma'am."

Jamie dropped her knife and pulled her sunglasses off. "Red?"

He nodded. "Paper bag on the floor."

She crossed the room, pulled out two big wineglasses and pulled the cork from the bottle, before pouring a little into each glass. "We may as well have fun, right? I don't mind waiting if we have something to do to pass the time."

Brett took the glass from her, wishing

he didn't have to look at her, that her eyes hadn't locked on his.

"To new beginnings," she announced, holding her glass up to touch his.

"Cheers to that," he said, wishing he'd been man enough to tell her how important the past was.

Brett took a sip as she did the same, swallowing the wine slowly before putting down his glass.

"So what do we do once we're done with chopping?"

They were standing side by side, Jamie with her glasses back on.

"If I was being a purist then I should have skinned the tomatoes first, but it'll still be great like this and otherwise we'll run out of time," he told her, pleased to take his mind off her by talking food. "We need to sauté the onions first with some fresh garlic, then add the tomatoes, some chopped red capsicum and a few handfuls of fresh basil."

"Sounds heavenly."

"Wait until you taste it with freshly shaved parmesan sprinkled on top with a grind of black pepper."

Jamie's tongue flicked out to moisten

her lips and he wished it hadn't. She was clearly thinking about the food, but it made his mind skip off in an entirely different direction.

"Sounds delicious."

"I also cheated with the pasta," Brett told her. "I should be making it myself, but I found a homemade spaghetti at the store."

"I can't believe *you're* teaching *me* a recipe."

He put down his knife and reached for the wine again. "You say that like I'm some uncouth caveman."

Jamie chuckled as she finished the onions and washed her hands. "I guess I just never took a special forces soldier for a cook. I mean, when have you even had time to learn culinary skills?"

"You did hear me say that I can only cook one dish from scratch, didn't you?"

"Yeah, but it's a damn good one from the sound of it," she said, pulling out a stockpot and turning on the gas. "Want me to start on browning the onions? I can be your sous chef if you like?"

He nodded and reached for the cloves of garlic he had sitting on the counter, then started peeling and slicing them. There was nothing he didn't like about cooking with Jamie, about being with her, about having her by his side.

Maybe it would have felt the same with any woman, because it wasn't like he'd ever cooked side by side with anyone else before, but deep down he knew he was kidding himself.

The way he felt for Jamie wasn't normal, which made it all the harder for him to fight. When he'd been out shopping, he'd wondered if he should just call her and say he'd gone back to his motel, that he'd see her again in a couple of days, but that thought had left his mind as fast as it had entered. Because Jamie was addictive, and right now, he was the addict.

"If we don't eat it soon my stomach is going to start roaring."

Jamie leaned back in her seat and gave Brett what she hoped was her most pathetic face. It seemed to work, because he laughed and walked himself and his glass of wine across the room and to the bubbling pot. The aroma of the sauce cooking had filled the room, and her stomach *was* starting to rumble.

"Mama will be shaking her fist up there in the clouds," he joked, turning around with the wooden spoon in his hand. "She'd be telling me that it needs two hours to reduce properly."

Jamie groaned. "I don't care." She took a final sip of wine and joined him in the kitchen. "Is this for me to taste?"

He nodded and held it out, his other hand poised beneath it to catch any drips.

"Tell me what you think," he said.

Jamie leaned closer and opened her mouth, letting him tip the spoon. The taste explosion made her shut her eyes for a second, instantly fuelling her angry appetite.

"Oh, my God," she managed to say after swallowing, her words all sounding like they'd merged into one. "That's incredible."

Brett dipped the spoon back into the pot and tasted a mouthful himself. "Not bad, if I do say so myself."

"I can't believe I've known you for so long and never known you could cook like that."

She reached for the spoon but he didn't let it go, shaking his head. "Just one more taste, then you have to wait until the pasta is cooked."

Jamie made a face but dropped her hand, waiting for Brett to offer her another mouthful. He was grinning when he extended it in her direction, before pulling back and leaving her openmouthed and waiting.

"Brett!"

He just laughed and gave it to her, but she moved at the same time, meaning a few drops dripped onto her chin. Brett pulled the spoon back and reached for her face, wiping gently at her chin, his fingers sweeping across her skin to catch the sauce. He licked the sauce from his finger, and she couldn't take her eyes from him, watching his face, his mouth, his tongue.

They were standing closer than they should have been, and now they were staring way longer than they should have been, neither blinking, just watching.

Brett moved his body slightly but Jamie stayed motionless, eyes still never leaving his. She couldn't think of anything else except for Brett; suddenly he seemed to fill the room with his presence. It was like he was towering over her, his body blocking out everything, his eyes stopping her from seeing anything else, his masculinity calling out to her, making her want to close the distance between them and end up wrapped in his big arms.

"Ah, I should put that pasta on, right?" he asked.

Jamie cleared her throat, took a step backward to put some distance between them, to force a space between them that would stop the magnetic pull she was feeling toward him. Toward a man she couldn't feel like that about, not yet. Not now. She'd lost two soldiers in her life already—there was no way she was going to let a third one break her heart.

"I'll, ah, go set up the table outside," she told him, nodding her head like she was trying to convince herself. "We may as well eat alfresco."

Brett turned away and pulled out a big pot, filling it with water and setting it to boil. "This won't take long. I'll bring it all out when it's ready."

Jamie swallowed a lump of something— maybe it was just pure emotion but it felt like pure pain to her—and pulled out place mats and cutlery. She could come back for the wine, but right now she needed some space. A moment to breathe. A moment to think about what she was so close to doing.

Because if she did it, if she gave in to her feelings, then there was no going back. And she didn't want to spend the rest of her life regretting ruining the one friendship that meant the world to her, and had meant even more to her husband.

Jamie walked outside and set the table, before wandering around to the side of the house and leaning against it, out of view of the kitchen. She needed to feel the air on her face, shut her eyes and just think.

About Sam. About the fact that she was still wearing her wedding ring, that she still loved the man she'd married five years ago, that she didn't want to be unfaithful to him even though he was gone.

And the fact that her feelings for Brett were starting to consume her.

Because friends or not, widow or not, she wanted to know what it felt like to kiss Brett again. To be held in his arms. To have his big body pressed against hers, protecting her, *loving her.*

"You okay?"

Jamie's eyes flew open and she smoothed her hands down over her shorts.

"Yeah, fine. I just needed a minute."

She turned to find him standing by the table, not coming into her space, but concern was written all over his face. He'd brought the wine and their glasses out, along with some napkins.

"Jamie, are we okay?"

She took a deep breath. "Yeah, we're okay." Jamie paused. "We are, right?"

Brett nodded, smiling, but his eyes told a story of concern. Of not knowing what to say, of what to think about what was happening.

Because they weren't okay and yet they were, all at the same time.

"How's that pasta looking?" she asked.

"Your stomach still growling?"

She reached for the wine bottle and poured a little more into each of their glasses. "It just so happens that I'm ravenous. I can't wait."

Brett gave her one last, long look before turning around and heading back inside.

"Give me two minutes. Then you can eat until you can't fit another mouthful in."

Comfort food was exactly what she needed, and if the taste of sauce she'd had inside was anything to go by, it might even take her mind off how she was feeling. At least for a few minutes.

CHAPTER SEVEN

JAMIE LEANED BACK, glass of wine in hand, staring up at the stars. It was only nine o'clock, but the sun had gone down long ago and the only light around them was the artificial kind. She'd lit the large candle in the center of the table, and the small flame was making her smile with its constant flicker against the glass, but it wasn't doing enough to distract her entirely from Brett.

Their dinner had been amazing, and things seemed to have simmered down between them. There had been no awkward silences, no difficult conversations, just a pleasant night eating alfresco in good company. She was full and content from the huge bowl of pasta she had, the tomato taste still lingering even now. She'd never tasted homemade tomato sauce like that, and now she had, she knew she'd never be satisfied with the bought kind again.

"You know, when you're away like we were, the stars are the only constant. The one thing you can look up at, and know that someone else in another country will be staring up at that same sky."

She turned her head slightly so she could see Brett's profile. The light was playing off his features, making him look even more handsome than usual. His dark hair looked black, shadows across part of his face making his features seem even stronger, more masculine. Jamie had always thought him handsome, but sitting out here with him tonight, watching the kind and thoughtful expressions on his face, she knew she'd never realized quite how gorgeous he really was. They'd spent so much time together over the years, but never alone like this without the other guys around.

"Did you wonder sometimes why you were there? Wish you weren't?" Jamie asked him. "I mean, it must have been hard dealing with being away so often, doing what you were doing."

He chuckled. "There were plenty of times

I wished I wasn't there, but that was usually because of boredom, or missing things from home." He paused, took a long sip of his drink, clearly deep in thought. "I never lost sight of why we were there, though. And without us? So many soldiers would have been losing their lives. There would be convoys blown up everywhere without our dogs detecting IEDs. Men coming home in body bags. The young guys standing on those bloody things is enough to make you physically sick. Just kids, in their twenties, and having to have prosthetic limbs fitted just to be able to walk again." He sighed. "And besides, the army was like my family. They were all I had."

"I can't even imagine what you went through. How you could put your life and your dogs in danger…" She froze, catching her lip between her teeth. "I'm sorry, I didn't mean…" Jamie wished she could have crawled into a hole and died. She knew why they did it, she just couldn't imagine dealing with it, living it. And she hadn't meant to bring up his dog dying again.

Brett smiled, but she knew the reminder of his dog must have hurt.

"It's okay, you don't have to worry about offending me," he said. "We all know the risks when we go in, but nothing prepares you. Especially for the hatred, of how desperate they are to blow each and every one of us into pieces. It's kind of hard to understand until you're there, and once you are, you just have to stay focused on the job."

"I heard about that dog they found. The one that survived despite everything she went through." Jamie sighed. "I should be embarrassed by how much I cried when I read it."

He laughed, his smile wide. "Yeah, she was injured, survived one of the harshest winters and summers on record, and managed to be spotted by troops more than a year later. Sarbi is the poster dog for never losing hope. And better still, she's an Australian citizen."

They sat in silence for a bit, and Jamie hoped she hadn't ruined the night by bringing up war and death. She'd been trying to avoid mentioning Sam, but somehow the conversation had reverted to soldier talk, which seemed to lead straight back to her husband.

"Do you think I'm going to make it? As a dog owner, I mean?"

Brett had been leaning back, his chair on two legs, but when she spoke he pushed in closer to the table and leaned toward her instead.

"Sweetheart, Bear is in love with you and you're desperate to look after him properly. If there was ever a partnership destined to work, it's this one. And besides, you were already doing well, it was just that he was a bit confused by your signals."

The smile that spread across her face was genuine, because if Brett thought she could make it, then maybe her chances weren't so bad after all. Especially with his help to make her understand her new canine—she wouldn't have ever given up on Bear, but they sure could have struggled for a while trying to figure one another out.

"Talking of partnerships," she said, digging her fingers into her palm to force herself to continue. "Are you sure I'm not keeping you from seeing anyone? I mean, I don't want you to feel that you have to be here babysitting me."

He stared at her, face expressionless. For

a moment she wondered if she'd offended him, wished she hadn't said anything, until he shrugged and grinned at her.

"I'm not seeing anyone, if that's what you're asking," he said. "And for the record, I have no plans to *babysit* you."

Jamie fought the blush that was heating her neck and cheeks, refusing to give in to it. "I didn't mean to be nosy, it's just you've been spending so much time with me, and I didn't want you to feel so sorry for me that you were missing out on seeing someone else. Someone…" *Special* was what she'd been thinking of saying. He might have said he wasn't seeing anyone, but it didn't mean he wanted to spend all his free time with her.

Now his expression was serious, completely different than before. "I'm not here because I feel sorry for you. Don't ever think that for a second."

She stared back at him, lost in his dark gaze, his eyes stormy and almost black in the half-light. She'd thought he looked beyond handsome before, but all riled up he looked even more irresistible.

"Don't get me wrong, I love having you here, but I feel guilty about keeping you from what you want to be doing," she said. "I know I need to stand on my own two feet, learn how to be alone." Just because she knew it, didn't make it any easier.

"Jamie, I only came back to Sydney for you."

She swallowed, not quite sure what to say. He wouldn't have come back to his home city if it hadn't been for her? Maybe she'd heard him wrong.

"I'm the one who should be feeling guilty, for taking so long to get back here. For not being here for you when you needed me," he said. "I've been beating myself up about deserting you for months, so believe me when I say that this is exactly the place I want to be. Sam was family to me, and that makes you family. I should have been here sooner."

"Oh, Brett, you were injured and you'd lost your best friend and your dog. You have nothing to apologize for," she told him. "I just appreciate seeing you again, having you here, but I wouldn't have judged you if you'd decided not to come home at all."

He cleared his throat, leaned across the table toward her and then seemed to change his mind, clasping his hands and staring back up at the sky.

"I didn't come back for no reason, Jamie."

When he looked back at her, she had to force herself not to hold her breath. Because she had a feeling that what he was struggling to tell her was something that would change *everything* between them. More than a touch or a drunken kiss ever could, which meant this was something she wasn't sure she wanted to hear.

Just because she was having feelings for him, knew that the way she felt about him had changed, didn't mean that she was ready to hear him admit the same to her.

"You don't need to tell me," she heard herself say, afraid..

"You know when we met, all those years ago? Before you had even met Sam?"

She did remember, well. It wasn't something they'd ever really discussed, but it wasn't something she'd ever forgotten, either. "You were dating that gorgeous blonde."

"She *was* gorgeous, but I finished with her that night."

Jamie felt her eyebrows pull together. "Why?" Now she *did* want to hear what he had to say. Why would any man end things with a woman that beautiful?

"Because after I met you, you were all I could think about. I didn't want to ask you out while I was involved, because I wanted to do it right, but by the time I found you…"

No, he couldn't have. Jamie gulped. "I was already with Sam," she finished for him.

"You were already with Sam," he repeated, "and he was happier than I'd ever seen him in his life, so there was no way I would have ever stepped in, even at the start. Sam was like my brother, and I'd have sacrificed anything for him. *And I did.*"

"But you were looking for me?" she said, voice low, almost a whisper. "You actually came looking for me after that night?"

"Yeah." He chuckled. "Kind of ironic, huh? It all just blew up in my face like I'd never even met you, like that night had never even happened."

"And you never told Sam? You just let us…" She didn't even know what to say.

The night she'd met Brett, at a party where she'd hardly known anyone, she'd been drawn to him immediately. But their flirting had been nothing more than that, because he'd had a girlfriend, although she'd be lying if she said she hadn't been thinking about him afterward. That she hadn't wished he'd been single.

And then she'd met Sam. Gorgeous, kind, loving Sam, who'd she fallen in love with and married within a year. Leaving Brett as a pleasant memory of what could have been.

"I told Sam that I'd never found the girl I met at that party, the one I'd talked about nonstop, because when I saw him with you, I knew he'd found *the one.*" Brett blew out a breath. "I never stopped kicking myself for letting you walk away that night, and I got to see my best friend marry my dream girl. And all these years I just kept my mouth shut and never said anything, because no good could ever have come out of me being honest about my feelings, about what had happened."

She couldn't stop staring at Brett, could hardly believe what he was telling her—the words that were coming out of his mouth. She'd been insanely attracted to him, too, but thinking about what could have been wasn't something she'd ever really considered, until now. Because she'd been happy with Sam, she'd *loved* Sam, and Brett had always been his best friend. His best friend who'd loved to flirt with her and make her laugh, who she'd always thought could have been someone more to her at a different time, different place.

"So what did you come back for this time, Brett?" she asked.

Brett shrugged. "I told myself I was coming back to look out for you, to stay true to what I promised Sam, but honestly? That's not the reason I'm still here."

Jamie's hand was shaking slightly as she reached for her glass, clutching the stem to steady it, for something to do to stop herself from staring at him. For the first time in her life, she was absolutely speechless—couldn't even grasp what he was telling her. She took a sip of wine.

"So why are you still here?" Her voice was so low she wondered if he'd even heard what she'd said.

"Because I've never forgotten how I felt that night I first met you, and how I felt every time I saw you with Sam over the past six years. Every single goddamn time, Jamie."

She'd be lying if she didn't admit to always liking him, too. Because the truth was, she'd never forgotten how she felt the night they'd met, either. And they'd always been so comfortable with one another, so easy.

"And how do you feel now?" she asked, feeling brave and needing to know how he honestly felt about her right now.

He reached for one of her hands, turned it so her palm was facing up and stroked his fingers across her skin before closing his hand over hers. "Honestly?"

Jamie nodded, needing to know, to hear what he had to say.

"I wish to hell I didn't feel so damn guilty, but my feelings for you haven't changed, and I don't think they ever will. No matter how many times I tell myself that it's wrong, all the reasons I have for it *to be wrong*, I can't change how I feel."

Which meant the ball was in her court. It was up to her to decide where this conversation was going, what would happen next. And just because she wanted something to happen, didn't mean she was ready for it.

"I…" Her voice trailed off. "I don't know what to say."

"Then don't say anything," he said. "Just

don't say anything, or forget I ever told you, if you need to. I don't want things to be weird between us, but I couldn't keep this to myself any longer."

"Do you ever think about what might have happened? What could have been if I hadn't met Sam, if you'd found me before then?" she asked, her voice almost a whisper. "Even the day before I met him, that could have changed everything."

"All the time," he said straight back. "I know things would have been different, but I was too slow to find you. We can't look back, Jamie. Trust me, I've been doing it for years and it's done nothing but infuriate me."

Jamie knew he wasn't going to make the first move—to him she was still Sam's wife, *forbidden*, out of bounds. He'd as good as told her that Sam had been the brother he never had, part of his surrogate family. But this was Brett. This was a man she'd loved as a friend for years, a man she could trust, and a man who was making her heart race like it hadn't in so long. A man whose arms, *lips*, she'd dreamed of; whose touch she'd often fantasized about. It was something she'd never admitted, but it was true.

She pulled her hand away from his and stood up, then slowly walked around the table to stand in front of him. She watched as he pushed back his chair a little, so he was facing her, the expression on his face hard to read. But his body language was more than obvious, telling her that he wanted her to come closer, that he wasn't going to say no. That he was ready and waiting for her to make a move.

Jamie moistened her lips, eyes on his as she closed the distance between them, arms hanging at her sides as she stared down at the man in front of her. She was going to bend down, had intended on sitting on his lap, but suddenly her confidence was waning. She wanted to be the confident, brazen woman who knew what to do and didn't hesitate, but it wasn't something she'd ever had to do before, especially after years of being with the same man.

Brett made it easier for her. He pushed up to his feet and now stared down at her, a good head or more taller than she was. Jamie placed her hands on his chest, feeling the heat of his body, the muscles of his body, through her palms. But it was nothing compared to the heat in his gaze.

She could hear her heart beating, her breath coming out in shallow bursts, but she wasn't going to back down, wasn't going to pull away when she was the one who'd started this. Brett was standing still, arms at his sides, but when she leaned into him, tilted her face up to him, his arms came up to circle around her waist and hold her.

They both hesitated, until her gaze hit his lips—his full, tempting mouth—and she suddenly couldn't wait any longer. Jamie stretched up, on tiptoes, lips meeting Brett's in a soft, luscious kiss that had her wrapping her arms around his neck to lock him in place.

She relaxed into him as he drew her closer, tucked tight against his big, warm body. Everything he'd just told her was running through her head, sending goose pimples down her arms and back at the thought of him wanting her all these years. And if she were honest, maybe she'd always felt the same, it just hadn't been something she would have ever acted upon. Until now.

"Jamie, are you sure about this?" Brett murmured, lips brushing hers as he spoke.

She nodded, arms still looped around his neck, and gazed up at him even though she was flushing all the way to her toes at the way he was looking back at her. Just because she was nervous didn't mean she wanted to shy away from how she was feeling— she wanted to enjoy it. Ever since Sam had died, she'd been lost, sad, alone. Brett was making her feel alive in ways she hardly remembered. It was like she'd become an old spinster, and now she was…well, now there was a fire back in her belly. It might have been wrong in so many ways, but at this moment, it was also right.

Jamie moaned as Brett kissed her again, his lips moving softly and then with more urgency, making her want to rip his clothes off him where he stood. She was conflicted, part of her unsure about being with another man, but the other part…? Maybe it was the wine giving her confidence, but Jamie wanted Brett like she hadn't wanted anything in a long time. And she'd barely consumed a glass, anyway.

She pushed up his T-shirt, wanting to

touch his skin, but his hands left her waist and closed around her elbows, stopping her.

"Hey," she whispered, mouth still firm against his.

"No," he said back, and she could feel his smile against her mouth.

Jamie dropped her hands, took a step back. "I'm sorry, I thought…"

He collected her hands and put them firmly back on his body, his arms looped around her waist again, and he tugged her closer.

"You thought right, I just think we need to take this slow," he said, mouth murmuring against hers. "Let's not rush into anything we could regret."

Brett tucked a finger beneath Jamie's chin, tilting it so she was looking up at him again. He could see the confusion swimming in her gaze and he didn't like that he was the cause of it.

"Sweetheart, you mean too much to me for us to ruin our friendship in one night. I'm trying to be the good guy here, and there are only so many times I'm capable of saying no."

She looked embarrassed. "You're, ah, right. I mean…"

He'd known Jamie a long time and he'd never heard her stutter, or be lost for words. But then he'd never been intimate with her, either.

"Jamie, look at me," he said, voice husky as he stared into her blue eyes.

She obliged, eyes finally locked back on his like she'd given in to the fact that she needed to watch him back.

"I meant everything I said, but I'm not even sure we should be doing this," he confessed. "I just don't want you to have any regrets."

Jamie sighed. "I know. You're right. It's just…" She blew out another breath. "Well, it's hard and confusing, but it also just seems natural. Like we're supposed to be doing this. It should feel wrong but it doesn't."

Brett smiled and dropped a slow kiss to her lips. "Don't take my being a gentleman as not wanting you, okay? Because if I had it my way I'd be dragging you to your bed and not letting you out of it until morning." He kept his lips only inches from Jamie's, teasing her. "Or maybe the next few days."

They both laughed, and he wrapped his arms around her for a proper hug, holding her tight. Brett inhaled the fresh orange scent of her shampoo, enjoyed the softness of her silky hair against his face, the feel of her slender body against his. He wasn't lying about wanting her, but he was also between a rock and a hard place.

Sam had been his best bud. He'd have taken a bullet for him, and if it had been a choice, he would have traded places with him in a heartbeat if Sam could have been alive to come home to Jamie. But now that he was here, with a lonely widow he'd been in love with for longer than he cared to admit, walking away, resisting her, was proving to be more difficult that he could have ever imagined. All he knew right now was that he was in love with a woman who should still be off-limits to him. And instead, he'd almost been at second base with her, and he'd had to stop things before they went a lot further, and fast. So much for being in control of his feelings.

"What do you say we head inside? Call it a night?" he suggested, even though it was the exact opposite of what he wanted to be doing. To what he was thinking.

Jamie nodded against his shoulder, but she wasn't letting go. Her arms were tight around him, face nestled against his neck.

"Am I a terrible wife?"

Her words were so low, such a whisper, that he wondered if she'd even meant him to hear them.

"You were a great wife, Jamie. But if you don't want something to happen here, it's your call." He wouldn't push her, and if she said no, then that would be the end of whatever had just happened between them. "I'll be here for you no matter what, okay? I want you to do what feels right for you. And I don't want us to do anything without thinking it through properly."

She didn't say anything, just kept holding on to him. When she finally stepped back, her hand came up to his face, warm against his cheek.

"You're a good man, Brett Palmer," she said, tears swimming in her eyes as she smiled up at him. *"The best."*

Brett just watched her, jaw clamped tight as he looked into her eyes. She was more than just a beautiful woman to him—she was a friend; she was Sam's widow; she was the woman he'd lusted after for weeks until he'd seen her in the arms of another man, then wondered every what-if about since. And now she was the woman he could have a chance with. *A second chance with.*

He cleared his throat, unsure of what she was trying to say. Was she letting him down softly, or the complete opposite?

"I think you're right, we need to call it a night," she said, her hand falling away as she stepped backward.

Brett nodded, but he quickly reached for her fingers before she moved too far, squeezing them before letting go.

"I'm going to stay out here a while," he told her, "clear my head a bit."

She grinned. "If you need any help with that, there's still almost half a bottle of wine sitting there."

He gave her a mock salute, smiling as she laughed and walked backward.

"'Night, Brett," she called out. "Oh, and thanks for the most delicious dinner I've ever eaten. You would have made your mama proud."

"Good night, Jamie," he said.

He watched as she glanced at Bear sitting under the table, but she didn't call out to him.

"You keep him for company," she said. "Just make sure he comes in before you go to bed."

Brett didn't take his eyes from her figure until she'd disappeared inside the house, and once she did, he poured himself a large glass of wine and sat down on the deck beside the dog. He would have preferred a beer, but wine would have to do.

"Do you think he'd kill me?" Brett asked the dog.

Bear raised his head and whined.

"Yeah, I know." Brett gave his head a rub before using that same hand to prop himself up. "He'd probably give me a black eye."

Sam wouldn't begrudge either of them happiness, but he'd only been gone six months and already Brett was moving in on his girl. And Jamie was more than Sam's girl, she'd been his *wife*. But he'd stood back once to let them be happy, done the right thing, and now maybe it was his turn. If something happened between them, if she really wanted it, then he wasn't going to push her away. Because he couldn't. And there was a part of him that thought maybe he finally deserved to be happy after everything he'd survived, that he needed to stop blaming himself for every bad thing that had happened in his life. That maybe he needed to accept that something good could happen to him....

The noise was deafening. The boom that hit his ears, the explosion, was still echoing in his head, until it started to ring—a high pitch that seemed to get louder and louder, and it was the only thing he could hear.

He picked himself up, staggered backward like he'd lost his balance, and realized his leash was still hanging from his hand. Only there was no dog attached.

He looked around him, tried to call out to his dog, but he couldn't hear his own voice. Then he saw the fur, parts of his dog's body. He was screaming but he still couldn't hear himself, just knew his mouth was open and his throat was raw, even as tears fell down his cheeks.

Sam. He couldn't see Sam either. He yelled out, spinning around and staggering, feet colliding. And then he realized Sam was gone. That the men back at the 4x4 were waving to him, he could see their mouths moving, and then he saw Bear. Sam's dog. He was dragging his leg, falling over, but Brett wasn't going to leave him. Couldn't leave him.

Then everything went black as arms reached out to him and he crashed to the ground....

Brett lay back on the deck and stared at the sky, trying so hard to fight the memories, to push them away and not go back to that dark place. There was nothing he could have done for Sam, he knew that. But he could do something about Jamie—he just had to figure out whether the right thing for her was having him around, or the exact opposite.

It would have been so easy for him to stop her from going to bed, to have asked her to stay with him for a while. It would be almost as easy for him to follow her, to take her hand and tell her how he really felt, tell her what he wanted, see if she wanted the same without offering her time to think about it. But something was holding him back, and he knew it probably always would.

Because no matter how good that kiss had been, no matter how much he wanted her in his arms, she wasn't his to want. She still wore her wedding ring, and she still loved her husband. So no matter what she might think or feel right now, he *needed* to give her time. Time to figure out what she wanted. He'd told her the truth, and now he just had to wait.

For some reason, he had to be the good guy around Jamie—he'd felt the same way that first night when they'd just met and spent hours chatting. There was something about her that brought out the good in him, and he liked it.

He just hoped that it was something about her house that had helped him sleep the night before. Otherwise? He'd have yet another reason to want her in his arms. It had been months since he'd been able to shut his eyes and just relax into blackness, to sleep without thinking, and he didn't want to go back to that dark place ever again. Not if he could help it.

CHAPTER EIGHT

JAMIE SAT ON her bed, legs curled up beneath her. She didn't know what to do. Part of her wanted to march straight back out to Brett and tell him that she'd often thought of that night they'd first met. Maybe not in recent years, but after she'd first been with Sam, she'd often wondered: *what if.* Sam had been the love of her life and she'd never for a moment *not* wanted to be with him, but Brett… well, Brett was Brett. He was a man she'd been physically attracted to from the moment she'd met him, and she'd also been charmed by him, too.

Until she'd realized that he had a girlfriend. A girlfriend she now knew he'd finished with so he could seek her out.

Argh. There was nothing about this that was easy.

Sam's smiling face, from a collection of their wedding photos, was staring at her from the dresser, a reminder to a life that no longer existed. A memory that would always make her happy, but one that wasn't a reality anymore. Just like her dad had become only a memory, so, too, would Sam. Because he was gone, and nothing she could do would ever bring him back.

But Brett was real. And he was sitting outside her house, on his own, instead of with her. Waiting for her to tell him what she wanted.

She uncurled her legs, stretched, then stood. She slowly walked toward the window and parted the blinds, knowing that she'd be able to see him. Sure enough, he was sitting where she'd left him, only now his arm was slung around Bear as he stared up at the sky. No doubt looking at the stars and remembering a time when he wasn't home, when things were different. Maybe he was even thinking about her.

Jamie longed to go to him, to be with him, but she didn't want to make a mistake with a man who meant so much to her as a friend— she'd be lost without him.

She touched her forehead to the window and watched him. Just stared at his silhouette—his broad shoulders, his dark hair, his muscled forearm resting over her dog—and the coolness of the glass gave her flushed skin some relief.

But instead of going to him, she went to her bedside table and pulled out her leather-bound notebook, the one she kept close in case she had an idea for a new story or illustration.

Suddenly she knew exactly what she needed to do. Jamie pulled the cap off her pen and tucked up under the covers, pen poised. When Sam had been away, they'd always written to one another. Even though they'd been able to talk via video chat, they'd written so they had something to look forward to, something to anticipate in the mail during the months when they were parted.

She needed to write to him now. Needed to get her feelings off her chest and tell him…how much she still loved him, but how much she needed to let part of that go so she could move on and be happy.

Dear Sam,
This is the only letter that I've ever writ-

ten to you, knowing it will never reach you. But part of me believes that you're still here, in some shape or form, and if you are, I need to tell you how I'm feeling.

I know in my heart that I will never stop loving you, no matter how much time passes or what happens in my life from this day forward. I know you'd be so proud of how Bear and I are getting along, and I wouldn't give him up for anything. But there's something I need to tell you, something I never thought would even be a possibility.

You've been gone now for just over six months, and Brett came to see me. I don't know how or why, but something has changed between us. I think I'm falling for him, Sam, and I need you to know that if you were here, this would never have happened. But you're not here, and Brett is, and I believe that you would want me to be happy. We're both holding back, stopping anything from happening, *because of you*, but I don't want to be alone just to prove to your memory that I loved you.

So I need you to know that I'm falling in love with your best friend. I trust him and I know he'd never to do anything to hurt me, and I need to see if we could be happy together.

I love you, Sam, with all my heart. Not a day goes past that I don't wish that you were still here, but I've had to accept that isn't ever going to happen. I always thought you were the one, but now I'm realizing that maybe there is more than one person out there in the world for each of us. I will never stop loving you.

Jamie xx

Jamie wiped away the tears that had spilled down her cheeks and ripped the page from her notebook, before folding the letter in half. She tucked it into an envelope, sealed it, then scrawled Sam's name across the front of it.

She had no idea if Brett would still be outside or not, but she needed to go to him before she lost her confidence. Because if she didn't act now, maybe she never would. And part of her believed that she deserved to be happy, no matter what.

* * *

Brett shut the door and locked it, before flicking the switch and plunging the living room into darkness. He'd sat outside feeling sorry for himself for so long that even the dog had tired of keeping him company, and now he needed to crawl into bed and just sleep. No amount of thinking, of questioning himself, was going to help him to make a decision, and now he just wanted to crash. Otherwise he'd just let old feelings of guilt start to seep back into his mind, and he was over dealing with the emotional baggage he'd carried for the last decade.

"Brett?"

He squinted into the dark, trying to figure out where Jamie was. Then she flicked on a light and he could see she was standing in the hall, facing the living room.

"Hey," he said, not having expecting her to still be up. "Did I wake you?"

She shook her head. "I never went to sleep."

Brett crossed the room but kept his distance, not wanting to tempt himself after the hard talk he'd been giving himself outside. Jamie was out of bounds and he had no intention of crossing that line again, no matter how much he wanted to. Unless she came to him, it wasn't even something he was going to consider. The ball was firmly in her court now, and he wasn't going to budge from *that* particular resolution.

"Can I, ah, get you anything?" he asked. He knew how stupid it sounded the moment he said it—what kind of question was that to ask somebody in their own house?

She didn't say anything, just stared at him. Why was she down here when she'd gone to bed almost an hour ago?

"Jamie, what happened before," he began, not sure how to tell her what needed to be said, what he'd been thinking about. "I'm sorry if I crossed the line, because I never meant to do anything to make you uncomfortable."

Jamie shook her head. "No, Brett, you didn't cross the line and you didn't do anything that I didn't want you to do. Sam is gone. We both know that, and we both need to understand what that means."

He swallowed, wishing this was easier, wishing he didn't feel the way he did about her. Because then he wouldn't be tempted by her lips, or her hair, or the way she was watching him.

"Jamie…"

"You said you'd be here for me, no matter what," she told him.

Brett never took his eyes off her, and he also never moved, even when she started to come closer.

"I meant that if you needed me…" he began, the rest of his sentence disappearing when her finger touched his lips to silence him.

"I need you, Brett," Jamie said, standing on tiptoe at the same time as she looped her arms around his neck. "I need you now. We can't punish ourselves for how we feel, because we're not doing anything wrong."

Brett never moved, kept his hands at his sides, scared of what would happen if he let himself touch her, if he gave in to what was so close to happening. He was only a man and if she pushed him there was no way he'd be able to walk away.

"Jamie…" he murmured, but he wasn't committed to telling her no, so he never did. He'd said if it was her choice then he'd let it happen, only he hadn't expected her to act quite so soon.

"Kiss me, Brett. That's what I need you to do."

He stared into her aqua-blue eyes, knowing he was a lost man. No amount of good intentions was ever going to be enough to resist Jamie, not when her body was skimming against his, her mouth so close.

Damn it! Brett's hands flew from his sides to her waist, locking her in place against him as he crushed his mouth to hers. Her moan only spurred him on more, made him yank her hard to his body, one hand leaving her hips to caress her back, to feel her long hair and fist into the soft curls.

"Jamie," he forced himself to say, his mouth hovering over hers, unable to back off even if he wanted to. "Are you sure? We can't go back from this. It changes everything."

She tipped her head back and looked into his eyes, her fingers tracing down his chest, before she grabbed hold of one of his hands and led him out of the room. Jamie flicked the switch in the hallway and walked them both to her bedroom, stopping at the door and leaning against the wall.

"I've never been so sure about anything, Brett," she whispered into his ear, her hand clutching his T-shirt tight to keep him near. "Take me to bed."

He stared at her, long and hard, before reaching past her and pushing the door open. There was only so long that he could play the good guy and keep telling her no. So what if he'd made himself a promise, if she was supposed to be forbidden? Jamie was holding his hand and inviting him to spend the night with her, and he'd lost all power to turn and walk away from her. This was her choice, and he wasn't going to try to change her mind. He'd told himself all along that he wouldn't fight it if she was sure it was what she wanted, if she came to him, and now she had.

Jamie laughed and walked backward into the room, holding both his hands. When she bumped into the edge of the bed, she stopped and pulled his hands around to settle on her waist again.

"Brett," she whispered, fingers stroking up and down his face, before she held onto his shoulders and reached up to kiss him again.

He broke the kiss only to push her back onto the bed, watching as she fell back before bending to settle over her, his thighs locking her in place as he straddled her. She reached out to him, pulling him down, but he needed a moment to drink in the sight of her—to see her long hair splayed out around her, her full lips facing him, the rise and fall of her breasts as she lay on her back beneath him. For years he'd wondered what it would have been like if things had been different, fantasized about having her in his bed, and now she was sprawled out beneath him.

Brett dropped his upper body over Jamie's, careful not to crush her with his weight, and kissed her mouth, before trailing kisses down her neck and back up to her lips again. For something that was meant to be so wrong, it felt so damn good.

"Don't stop," she whispered, sounding breathless.

He chuckled, smoothing the hair from her face before stroking her cheek. "I have no intention of stopping," Brett told her.

"Good," she replied, claiming his mouth

again as she cupped his skull to force his head down, gripping on tight, fingers twisted in his hair.

Her lips moved gently, her tongue exploring tentatively at first, before becoming bolder, colliding with his.

All the best intentions in the world couldn't have made him say no to this.

Jamie let Brett push her T-shirt up and she wriggled out of it, left in only her bra and her shorts. She gulped when he immediately reached down for her button, before unzipping the denim and pulling it down her legs—slowly, as if he were trying to tease her. She pointed her toes so he could slip off the jeans completely, and laughed.

"Why do I have all my clothes off, and you're fully dressed still?" she asked.

He grinned and shrugged, but she wasn't going to let him sit there in his jeans and T-shirt while she was left in only her underwear.

"Off with it," she ordered, pushing his T-shirt up, eyes feasting on his stomach and chest muscles.

Brett obliged, taking it off and then standing to shed his jeans, too.

She sucked back a big breath as she watched him, looking at his big body, eyes glued to him as he lowered himself back on the bed. Jamie reached out to touch the tattoo on his left arm first, and then his other shoulder, fingers tracing over both of them. Years ago, she'd hated tattoos, but she'd grown to appreciate them now. And Brett's ones meant something to him, told a story of who he was and what was important to him, and the ink stretched over his muscles gave him a tough edge that was at odds with how gentle and kind he'd always been to her. If ever she needed reminding of the soldier he was, of how he could protect her if ever she needed it, his tattoos made that crystal clear.

Jamie slipped her hands onto his shoulders to stroke her nails down his back, but his whole body tensed, went rigid.

"What's wrong?" she asked, dropping her hands, knowing that he hadn't even remotely liked the way she'd just touched him.

Brett gave her an unconvincing smile. "My back's kind of off-limits," he said.

"You mean because of your injuries?" she

asked, voice soft, knowing how difficult it must be for him to talk about.

"Yeah."

"You don't have to be embarrassed, Brett," she said, leaning up to press a kiss to his shoulder, gently touching his lower back this time and avoiding where she'd almost touched before.

"Jamie..." He said her name as if it were a warning.

But she wasn't going to take no for an answer, not after all they'd been through together. She wanted to touch every part of Brett, and she wasn't scared of what had happened to him or the marks that had been left on his skin. It wasn't like they'd just met and he had to hide who he was from her.

"Let me see you," she whispered, pushing him gently back down to the bed. "There's nothing I could see right now that could change the way I feel about you."

CHAPTER NINE

CHILLS RAN UP and down Brett's body just at the mention of his scars, of her seeing them. He hadn't let anyone other than the medical team that had worked on him see how he looked now, to really see what had happened to him. Jamie looking at the mess that was his skin wasn't something he ever wanted to happen, but the way she was staring at him, like he was doing something to hurt her by not just opening up, was telling him that he may not have a choice. He didn't want to hurt her, had no intention of pushing her away, but this was something that he needed to prepare for.

"I can't," he muttered, rolling firmly on to his back.

Jamie tucked her knees up to her chin and wrapped her arms around her legs. The mood had changed, was no longer about sex and suddenly included a whole lot of stuff that Brett wasn't ready to face. Gone was the fun, flirty vibe they'd had happening between them, replaced by a serious, we-need-to-talk session.

"You've never talked about…"

"And I don't want to," he said, voice firm as he interrupted her. There was no way he was going to start talking, not now. That he was going to ruin what had been an otherwise perfect evening by dredging up exactly how his skin had become so disfigured.

"Can we just pick up where we left off?"

"You don't need to tell me, Brett, but let me see. *Please?*" she asked.

He shut his eyes, not wanting to get angry with this woman who'd been through so much, who he so genuinely cared about. Who was being so brave in another way that he knew must be beyond difficult for her. It shouldn't be so impossibly hard, but it was. Opening up had always been difficult for him, yet he'd told her openly about the truth of his past, about his parents and how he still felt responsible for their deaths.

This, though…this was different. The pain was too fresh.

"I'm embarrassed," he admitted, opening his eyes and looking straight into hers. "I'm no longer the guy who can go to the beach and just take off his top without thinking about it. It's not something you want to see or hear about. It's not who I am. And it's not how I want you to see me."

Now it was Jamie shaking her head, telling him he was the one in the wrong. "No, Brett," she told him, voice low and husky. "You *are* still that guy, because you're still handsome and you're still *you*. I don't care what your skin looks like, but we can't do this without you opening up to me. We can't take this further if there's any secrets between us."

He knew he was being stupid, that there was no point in delaying the inevitable, but letting Jamie see what he'd been through, what he was *still* going through, was like giving up a piece of his soul that he'd never intended on letting anyone be witness to. His skin had always been tanned and blemish-free, he'd always been the one to whip his shirt off on a hot day, but everything had changed the day he'd been burned. And not just his body, but his mind, too.

"It's ugly," he said, voice flat, knowing he was fighting a losing battle.

"I don't care," she said straight back, her gaze unwavering. "I just want you to let me in, Brett."

Jamie dropped her arms and moved closer, hands on his shoulders as she gently motioned for him to move. She couldn't have made him budge an inch if he hadn't wanted to, but he knew that the only way Jamie was going to trust him, that they were going to move past this, was if he let her in. If he trusted her to see what scared him the most.

Brett took a deep breath and reluctantly rolled over onto his stomach, hands under his chin as he lay there for her to inspect him. He was expecting a gasp, something to tell him what a shock it was for her seeing him like that, but all he could hear was silence. A long stretch of silence that had him holding his breath, wishing he'd refused.

And then she touched him. Brett dropped his head into the pillow. He'd been waiting for her to make a noise and now he was the one forcing back a groan. Or maybe it was a cry for help, he didn't know—all he knew was that Jamie was touching him in a way that was making him want to scream at her to stop, and at the same time beg her never to take her hands off of him. Because now she'd seen it, there was no going back, and all of a sudden he wanted her to see the real him. Needed her to see his pain and help to heal him, because he didn't want to be broken anymore.

Her fingers traced his entire back, dipped into the tender areas where he'd almost been burned alive, before she caressed the smooth parts of his back that reminded him of what all his skin had once looked like. What his body had once been.

Then she started to trace down his leg, too, the leg that he was so lucky to still have attached to his body, but that was disfigured from the skin grafts he'd painfully endured in recovery.

"Stop," he commanded, head rising off the pillow. His back was one thing, but she was taking things too far.

"No," she whispered, pushing him back down and straddling his buttocks instead.

He still had his boxers on, but he could feel the heat of her as she sat on him. "Don't move a muscle."

Jamie put her palms over Brett's arms as he spread them out on either side of him. At the same time she dipped her head until she could press a soft, warm kiss to his back, between his shoulder blades. Here, the skin was still smooth and tanned, like his back had always been, and she wanted to start here before she moved lower.

"Jamie…" She heard him mumble her name.

She continued undeterred, moving her mouth slowly down his back. When she reached the first of the jagged edged lines that crisscrossed down his entire lower back, she made her kisses even lighter, only just letting her lips touch him, as soft as she could make them. His skin was still pink where he'd been burned, the marks a blazing reminder of what he'd been through, and she needed to show him that she didn't care, that she could deal with the wounds he'd come home with, the wounds that he'd be forced to live with forever. That she accepted the man he was today as much as she would have accepted the man he'd been before the explosion—that in her eyes he was no different.

Her hair fell forward and splayed across his back as she started to move lower again, making her way down his leg now, shuffling her body farther down the bed. His right leg was impossible to compare to his back—the scars extended all the way down his thigh and calf, enough to make her want to gasp, at least when she'd first seen them. But now she focused on the shape of his leg, the muscles still bulging from his calf, the thickness of his thigh that told her how fit he was, how determined he'd been to stay strong even through what must have been a painful recovery. Brett was a fighter, she knew that, and he'd endured what might have broken others.

"They're just marks, Brett," she told him as she wriggled back up his body and sat on his buttocks again, hands spread out over his back as she gently massaged his shoulders.

"They're marks I'll have forever," he muttered.

When he went to move, she pushed herself up on her knees so he could flip onto his back beneath her. Jamie lowered herself when he looked comfortable, staring into his eyes as she leaned forward. She tucked her long hair behind her ears to keep it out of the way.

"You're still the same, handsome Brett you were to me before I saw them," she said. "It's part of you now, and they don't scare me."

"You have to say that now," he told her. "You can't exactly be honest with me about how much they disgust you."

Jamie frowned. "Of course I can be honest with you." She paused, touching his cheek with the tips of her fingers because she needed to connect with him, needed him to know that she was telling the truth. "Do your scars terrify me and remind me of what we've both lost? Sure. But they're just marks, Brett, and they're *your* marks, so there's no point in pretending like they're not there. Now that I've seen them, I've seen them. You don't have to worry about hiding them from me, or how I'll react."

"I hate that I have a constant reminder on my skin," he admitted, reaching up for her and stroking a hand down her hair until he reached the ends of it, skimming the center of her back.

"At least you're alive to be reminded of it," she whispered. "At least you're here, right now, in my bed."

Brett groaned, his hand falling from her hair. "I'm sorry, I…"

"Shhhh," she said, leaning down on to him, her elbows on either side of his head to prop herself up, bodies pressed together. "Stop talking."

"And what?" he asked.

"Kiss me again."

Jamie didn't wait for Brett to act, because she was already hovering above him, lips aching to close over his and feel what it was like to be almost naked and this intimate with a man she'd been attracted to for so long. *And he didn't disappoint.* Brett's mouth was firm against hers, his lips warm and soft. His hands were in her hair as she pressed herself even tighter against him, her body tight to his.

She could feel how much he wanted her, and it only made her sure in her decision. Brett wasn't just some rebound guy to her, someone to fill the bed with to keep her warm. He was a man she already cared so much about, only now…

"Jamie, I think we need to slow this down," he said, hands still tangled in her long hair as he yanked her back a little.

"No," she told him, wriggling against him until he groaned, fighting him. "Don't stop."

Jamie was being cruel to him, she knew she was, because he was trying to be the good guy and she was the one lying on top of him, forcing him into compliance. Making him be bad. But she didn't want him to be the good guy right now, didn't want him to think at all, she just wanted him to act.

"Are you sure?" he mumbled in between kisses.

"I've never been so sure about anything in my life," she whispered, before claiming his mouth again and teasing him with her tongue. There was no way she was going to let him stop.

Brett's moan was all she needed to spur her on, to make her reach behind her back and fumble to unhook her bra. His expert hands came to her assistance, and all of a sudden they were completely skin-to-skin, her breasts against his warm chest, almost as close as two people could be.

"This feels right," she told him, pulling back so she could look into his eyes. "Don't you think?"

From the way he was staring back at her, she knew he felt the same. It was different, it was terrifying, and it was exhilarating, because it was the first time she'd been intimate with a man who wasn't her husband in six years, *but it was Brett*. And if there were ever going to be another man besides Sam she made love to, she knew in her heart that it was right that man was him.

CHAPTER TEN

JAMIE WOKE UP and reached out an arm, feeling for Brett, but she opened her eyes instead because there was no warm body beside her. She sat up, pulling the sheet up with her to cover her breasts, and she spotted him straight away. He was sitting in the big armchair she had beside the window, his T-shirt and boxers on, staring at something that she couldn't see. Or maybe he was just staring at nothing.

"Hey," she said.

Brett turned, his big body filling the entire chair that had always seemed so roomy to her when she tucked her legs up and read a book in the sun.

"Morning," he replied.

Jamie watched the way he looked at her, like he wasn't sure, like something was troubling him. His expression was nothing like the one she'd witnessed before they'd fallen asleep.

"Brett, what's wrong?"

He shoved a hand through his hair. "You want me to be honest?"

She knew there was only one answer she could give to that question. "Yes."

He sighed. "Everything."

Tears pricked her eyes and she blinked them away, refused to let them even come close to spilling. After last night, she'd expected to wake up in his arms, thought what they'd shared was special, that they'd just pick up again where they'd left off, but the way he was looking at her...

"I don't understand," she managed to say, eyes never leaving his.

She watched as Brett stood and crossed the room, moving to the bed beside her. A low moan from Bear made her gaze flicker for a second, but the dog was still in his own bed.

Brett took one of her hands, the other still clutching the sheet and keeping her covered. All of a sudden she felt vulnerable being naked, whereas before she'd been completely comfortable.

"I feel guilty," he admitted, fingers stroking the back of her hand as he held it. "I don't want to, but I can't help it."

She understood the guilt, but if he was having second thoughts about what they'd done... "Brett, I don't regret last night, if that's what you're worried about. Not for a moment."

He moved closer, his thigh pressed to hers as he faced her. "I don't regret it, either, but what we did, what happened, it's changed everything."

"Is that the worst thing in the world?" she asked.

He smiled, but the sadness in his eyes scared her.

"If I'm honest with you, I can't think of anything I'd rather do than be with you. For the first time since the explosion, I've slept through the night, like I'm protected in your arms from the worst of my memories. And then I wake up and realize that I've taken Sam's place, that I've taken something from him, and it scares me."

She took a deep, shuddering breath. "If

Sam was here, this never would have happened, Brett," she told him, her voice barely more than a whisper. "But we are here, together, and somehow we're helping each other through. Can't we just enjoy being together without feeling guilty?"

He nodded. "I've always thought of you as part of my family, Jamie. I guess I just don't want to be responsible for losing another family member."

Jamie touched his cheek, let the sheet fall away to her waist. "You're not going to lose me, Brett. I promise. But I'm also not going to lie to you and say that I don't love Sam still, because I do. So much. But the way I feel for you…"

"We can't," he insisted.

"We can," she said firmly, not about to let them ruin what had happened because they were afraid. Because he was scared of losing something that he wasn't even in danger of losing.

They stared at each other, and she knew how hard it was for him because it was just as hard for her.

"You're not betraying Sam."

"If sleeping with his wife isn't betraying him, then I don't know what is."

"Come here," Jamie said.

He looked like he was going to resist, but he obeyed, moving closer. It wasn't that he didn't want to be with her, she knew that, but she also understood that his morals could ruin what was so fragile, so new, between them right now.

"Take off your top and get under the covers."

Brett went to protest but she shook her head before he could say anything. "Just do it for me, please."

He followed her instructions and pulled the covers up over them both, but he still looked awkward. Jamie pushed him down on the pillow then lay her head on his chest, arm around him.

"I need this, Brett. After last night, I can't deal with arguing or not having you here beside me. Because then I might start to feel guilty about what we did, and I've accepted the decision I made."

She listened to his breathing, focused on the inhale and exhale of air and the way it made his chest move.

"I don't want to hurt you," Brett told her.

She traced circles on his skin, fingertips needing to touch. "You won't hurt me, Brett, and I won't hurt you. But if you walk out on me? That will hurt. Because I don't want last night to have meant nothing. If we're talking about betraying Sam, then that would be it."

"As in you don't want what we did to be a one-night stand."

"I don't want it to be a one-night anything," she admitted, moving so she could rest her chin on his chest and stare at him. "What we did wasn't because of loneliness or selfishness, it was because it felt right, and I know you feel the same."

Brett reached for her hair, stroking it. "I just don't feel right, being in this room, seeing the photos of him, knowing that I've just stepped in and somehow taken over his life. Slept in his bed with his wife. It's not okay."

Jamie smiled at him, needing him to be honest with her, needing to hear the words that he'd been holding trapped inside.

"You stepped in to look after me, and what happened between us? It just happened. But if you want me to…"

"You're not taking down his photos because of me."

She laughed at the seriousness of Brett's tone. "I'm not taking down any photos, but what I was going to say is that we can always stay in the other bedroom. If you need to, I mean."

Brett groaned. "Can we just go out for breakfast? Walk somewhere?"

"You bet," she said, leaning forward to kiss him.

What started as a light peck became deeper, their lips moving softly, brushing together, before Brett cupped the back of her head so she couldn't get away, mouth more insistent.

"It doesn't seem to matter what I tell myself," he muttered, breaking the kiss, "I just can't get enough of you."

"Breakfast," she told him, pushing herself up and dragging the sheet with her so she could escape to the bathroom without him seeing her naked in the bright light. "Before we end up staying in bed all day."

It wouldn't have been a bad thing, but they both needed to get out of the house. There were too many memories in this room that were haunting Brett, and if she were perfectly honest, in the full morning sunshine, there was something not so easy to ignore about being with another man in the room she'd shared for years with her husband. No matter how much she wanted it to feel right, she knew that going out was exactly what they needed to do. A quick shower and a little makeup and she'd be ready to go.

She'd already been through losing her father, and then as good as losing her alcoholic mom for years at a time. So losing Sam and then losing Brett? Not something she had any intention of letting happen, especially not now that they'd spent the night together.

Brett clipped Bear's leash on and dropped to his haunches, looking the dog in the eye as he ran his fingers through his fur. He missed his own dog like crazy, was so used to having a constant companion by his side.

"You're doing pretty well with everything that's going on," he told the canine.

He received a low whine from Bear in return.

"It might not be guns and explosives, but it's still tough, huh?"

"Are you talking to yourself or the dog?"

Brett cleared his throat when he realized Jamie had walked into the room. "The dog, of course. Talking to myself would just be weird."

"He saying much in response?" she teased.

Brett looked her up and down, knowing there was no way he'd ever be able to resist her so long as he was staying in the house with her. When he wasn't with her, he was thinking about her, and when he was with her...*damn*. No amount of good intentions would ever help him when they were together.

"Let's go," he said, before he had any longer to think about Jamie and the way she was making him feel.

"Are we going to walk all the way there?"

He laughed. "You make it sound like it's a hike."

"I'm the girl who always takes a car. You seem to keep forgetting that."

"You have a dog now, and a guy with you who likes to feel like he's earned a cooked breakfast. So Bear and I vote for the walk, that's you outnumbered."

Jamie sighed and took Bear's leash from

him, smiling as their hands collided. "My dog, remember? I'm the one who's supposed to be up for walking all the time."

Bear was looking up at them, studying them each in turn, and he felt sorry for the poor dog, listening to them banter. There was no chance he'd ever figure out what they were saying, and he'd been so used to understanding commands when he'd been on the leash for work.

"He's all yours, let's go."

Brett waited for her to shut and lock the door behind them, before walking slow to match her pace. The sun was shining down on them already, another hot Sydney day. He'd spent days and weeks out under the scorching sun, working with his dog and the other guys, patrolling for explosives constantly, but that sun had never been enjoyable. It had drained them all and made them grumpy, made their skin dry and their throats burn. This sun made him feel free. *Alive.*

"Brett, I know you don't want to talk about what happened...."

He glanced sideways, seeing the frustrated look on Jamie's face as she clearly tried to figure out how to talk to him about something she was obviously so desperate to know more about. It wasn't that he didn't want to talk to her, it was just that dredging up the past wasn't always worth the pain, or the reality. He'd been in a black hole that could have swallowed him alive, his thoughts so dark they'd almost consumed him, and going back wasn't good for him or her.

If he shut his eyes, he could still smell the burned flesh, still feel the searing pain of the fire as it shot up his leg and across his back.

"I just…" She paused and stopped walking, arms crossed like she didn't know what to do with them. "I just want to know if it happened fast? If he suffered. I'm sorry." She blew out a big breath. "I've been wanting to ask someone that question for so long, and I think you're the only one who can answer it because everyone else just wants to fob me off and pretend like it wasn't anywhere near as horrific as I know it was."

Brett started walking again, because if he

was going to talk then he needed to keep moving, needed something else to focus on to help him say the words. He'd thought she wanted to know about his experience, what he'd been through, but she wanted to know about Sam and he could hardly hold that back from her. She deserved to know.

"When we were working that day, it was just like usual," he began, wondering how the hell he was going to say what he needed to say, but continuing anyway. It wasn't something he'd ever talked about, but it was a scene that had run though his head constantly ever since it had happened. He could see it as if it were yesterday—shut his eyes and pretend like it was that day all over again. "We were with a unit of SAS guys, providing support, and I was working with Sam. We both got our dogs out and started doing our drill, but we knew there was something off almost immediately."

He was staring straight ahead when Jamie slipped her hand into his, and he didn't resist. Because talking about that day was beyond hard, and it was something he'd never done before. Brett needed her strength.

"His dog identified the explosive immediately," he continued, ignoring her because now he'd started talking he needed to get it all out. "His dog went dead still, and for a split second we looked at one another, because we knew it was bad, that we were in a hot spot, that Bear had only frozen like that for one reason. We called out to the guys not to move, and then Teddy indicated another one." He paused. "You have to understand that sometimes, most of the time, our dogs just raise their tails slightly, move differently, in a way that only their handler would ever notice. But we all knew what Bear had detected that day, and we all knew how badly things could end. That we might never see another day."

Brett swallowed down the lump of emotion choking his throat and blinked to force the tears back. He didn't want to cry, didn't want to *feel* again, but the memories were crashing into him like they'd only just happened.

Jamie was squeezing his hand tight, like she wanted to take some of the pain for him, but he knew she already had enough pain of her own to deal with. He just wanted to tell her like it was, explain to her what had happened so they could both move forward and never have to talk about it again.

"From that moment, it was like everything moved in slow motion, before becoming such a fast blur that I don't even remember the details." He looked at her, saw that Jamie's eyes were filled with tears, just like his were from going back in time to that day. "All I know is that I was blown back so far my body was slammed down close to the 4x4, and Sam was gone. So was Teddy. To this day, no one can understand how Bear managed to survive the blast, or how either of us didn't lose limbs. But it was fast, so fast that I don't know how or why I ended up so far from the bomb."

Jamie's hand in his stopped him from moving as she pulled him to a halt. She had the leash in her other hand, and she let go of Brett's hand for a second so she could loop her arm around his neck and draw him into an embrace so warm, so loving, that he was powerless to pull away. *And he didn't want to pull away.* Because no matter how guilty he felt, this felt so right, too. He needed Jamie as much as she needed him. He liked that he could be honest with her when he needed to be, that they understood what the other had gone through, on some level at least.

"Thank you for telling me," she murmured, pressing a kiss to his cheek. "Thank you, for being honest with me when no one else could."

Brett shut his eyes. Sam's blood covered him, bits of his best friend burning and blasted all around them. There were so many pieces of him, so much flesh that when Brett had woken up, he'd vomited until there was nothing left in his stomach. And his dog, his beautiful dog had been killed on impact, too.

But they weren't memories he was ever going to share with her. If he ever needed to get them off his chest, he could tell Logan, a fellow soldier who'd seen enough on his tours to cope with what he'd hear. He'd never let Jamie suffer through those particular memories with him, the blatant truth of that day. There were some things she needed to be protected from, and that was top of the list.

Jamie pulled back then, looked into his

eyes and didn't break contact even as she kissed him.

"I need you to know that I want you here, Brett. It might be weird, that we're together and all that, but all I know is that this is right. That having you in my life seems right and I don't want to lose you."

He nodded, but he still wasn't convinced that what they were doing was any part of okay or right. It wasn't that he didn't have feelings for Jamie, because he did. His problem was that he felt too much for her, and he knew that he'd never, ever want to walk away. That this wasn't just about comfort or friendship.

"When you say you want me here, do you mean that we keep this just between us, or...?"

She ran her hand down his arm before looping it through so they could walk arm in arm. "I think we should tell Logan. I mean, I don't want to lie to him and I don't want to come between your friendship. We need to be honest with him."

Brett blew out a breath. "Logan is not going to be okay with this."

"I know, but we need to tell him. *I'll tell*

him. I just don't want this to be any more awkward than it needs to be, and the longer this goes on, the harder telling him will become, because he'll think we've been lying to him all along if we don't come clean."

"Maybe we should text him, tell him to meet us for lunch or something after our walk tomorrow?" Brett suggested. "He might take it better if there's a lot of people around. You know, so he can't knock out every tooth in my mouth." After the way Logan had warned him off the other night… it wasn't going to be pleasant, no matter how or where they did it. Logan was going to be furious, not with her, but with him.

Jamie laughed but he shook his head.

"What?" she asked.

"I don't think you know Logan like I do," he said. "There is nothing about this that's going to be easy. He's like a teddy bear around you, acts like he wouldn't hurt a fly, but the Logan I know isn't going to deal with this well."

"I lost my husband, Brett, and now something has happened between us. I'm not intending on acting like you've taken advantage of me, if that's what you're worried he'll think."

Logan was going to kill him. Actually kill him.

Jamie couldn't stop laughing as Bear ran after the stick she'd just thrown like his life depended on it. Having fun with him had changed the dynamic between them, and she was pretty sure her dog was enjoying it as much as she was.

"I told you, he made the squad based on his determination with balls and sticks," Brett said, grinning straight back at her.

"Why did I never realize how much fun he was before?"

Brett came up and put his arm around her. "Because you were both trying to figure the other out, and everything had become too serious. It was like a child living with you who wasn't allowed to have fun, so he was bored and didn't understand what was being asked of him."

Jamie gave Bear a hearty pat when he dropped the stick at her feet for the umpteenth time. "Good boy," she praised, before throwing it again.

"We used to call Bear the branch manager and my dog the deputy branch manager," Brett said, pressing a kiss to her cheek. "The two of them used to have a blast when we let them play."

Jamie leaned into Brett, enjoying his arm around her and the sun beating down on her shoulders. She moved only when he had to reach into his back pocket to retrieve his mobile.

"Is it Logan?" she asked.

Brett tapped a message into his phone before turning his attention back to her. "Yeah. He's said yes to lunch tomorrow."

"What do you say we just grab something to take away this morning?" she asked him, shaking her head at Bear as he faithfully retrieved the stick again. He looked disappointed that their game was over, but it wasn't like they hadn't let him have a heap of fun. "I know a place nearby where they do a mean bacon-and-egg sandwich, and we can sit in the sun and relax."

Brett's gaze met hers. "That's exactly what I need to take my mind off things."

"You mean Logan?" she asked, tucking

under his arm and pulling him along with an arm around his waist.

"Yeah." He hugged her back as they walked. "So where is this amazing food place?"

"Ah, it's more like a food shack, but I promise you it's good. They do great coffee, too."

"So it'll kind of be like our first actual date?" he asked, raising an eyebrow when she looked at him.

"Yeah, I guess it will be. That okay with you?"

"Sure is. But I'm guessing we might have to buy for Bear, too. I doubt he's going to tolerate us eating greasy food in front of him without sharing."

Brett knew he needed to just shut his mind off, but it was easier said than done. Meeting Logan was seriously playing with his head, and he knew better than Jamie how tomorrow was going to go down. But there was nothing he could do about it right now, so he needed to shake off his worries.

"My shout. Want the same as me?"

Brett returned her smile, not wanting to

ruin her happiness. "Whatever's good, but order me two."

"Typical boy," she muttered, spinning around to go in and order.

He watched as she disappeared then came back with a number on a piece of brown paper.

"Oh, this is a really classy place, isn't it? I was thinking of taking you somewhere nice for our first date, not to a takeaway joint."

She giggled. Jamie actually giggled, and the noise was infectious enough to make him laugh straight back at her.

"Trust me, it's worth overlooking the surroundings for the food. And the coffee. Did I mention the coffee?"

"I think you're being paid to do PR for this place," he said to her, grabbing her hand and pulling her in against his body. "I don't believe you for a second."

"Well, you should," she whispered, tipping her chin up and brushing her lips against his.

She jumped away when their number was called. Brett couldn't take his eyes off her as she walked away—and he couldn't have forgotten her smile even if he walked away and never returned. Jamie was getting under his skin, and there was nothing he didn't like about it.

"Here you go," Jamie announced as she emerged once again. "Coffee for you, and the food is wrapped up in here. Let's go find a spot somewhere nice."

They walked the five minutes back to the park and sat on the grass, Bear sprawling out beside them. Jamie reached into the bag and pulled out massive sandwiches wrapped in paper, passed one to him, then unwrapped one for Bear and put it on the ground, before taking one for herself.

"Well, it at least smells good," he told her, taking his first bite.

She did the same, watching him, like she was expecting a reaction. He took another bite, and ketchup and sauce oozed out down his hand, along with runny egg yolk that tasted incredible.

"Amazing or what?" she asked, eyebrows raised as she kept eating hers, hands tilted up to keep the sauce from running onto her skin.

"You win, it's amazing," he told her, mouth full as he tried to talk. He kept eating, not able to stop for the juice running out of it.

When they'd both finished and cleaned up as best they could, using only paper napkins, Brett lay back on the grass beside Jamie, his elbow propping him up. He looked at Jamie, and she at him, both nursing their coffees.

"Thanks for this," he said, reaching out to run his hand down her hair, tucking a few loose strands behind her ear.

"For greasy food and damn good coffee?" she teased.

"No, for showing me that we can just hang out and enjoy being together. That it's simple things like this that are important, just…" He didn't even know what he was trying to tell her. "I guess what I'm really badly attempting to say is that being with you isn't easy for me, but it's worth it. It's worth the pain just to have you with me."

Jamie brushed the back of her fingers against her eyes, and it was only then he realized that she was trying to disguise her tears.

"Don't cry, Jamie. Please don't cry," he murmured, taking her hand and squeezing it tight.

"Just ignore me, I'm all emotional," she said, smiling and squeezing his hand back. "I'm happy, Brett, I promise you I'm happy."

"Good. If you're happy, then I'm happy."

And it was true. He might be finding being with Jamie hard to wrap his head around, to deal with, but her being happy was what was important.

CHAPTER ELEVEN

THE SUN SHONE brightly through the window and onto Jamie's face as she struggled to open her eyes. She reached out a hand and found an empty space beside her again, which was the only reason she forced herself to sit up, to see if Brett was sitting across the room in the chair again.

He wasn't. But when she glanced toward the door, he was standing there watching her.

"What are you doing up so early?" she mumbled, dropping back down into the pillows but not taking her eyes off of him.

He laughed, crossing the room and carrying a large tray. "First of all, it's almost nine o'clock, so it's not early, and second, I was getting you breakfast."

She pushed herself back up again and flattened the bedding out so he could put the tray down.

"Did you make this?"

Brett chuckled again. "No, I took Bear for a run and picked it all up at that place down the road. Turns out they do fresh fruit salads and muffins for people like me. All I had to do was put them on a plate and walk them upstairs for you."

She leaned in for a kiss. "Well, it's the thought that counts. And I'm starving."

Brett carefully settled himself across from Jamie, obviously trying not to tip the tray, and reached for a bowl of fruit. "It scares me to even say it, but I could get used to this. Being with you, the whole domestic bliss routine."

When she smiled he grinned straight back at her. "Me, too," she said. "But maybe you'll feel differently when you realize I'm not *that* domestic."

"When I say domestic, I wasn't exactly referring to housekeeping."

Now it was Jamie laughing at him, waving a piece of fruit on a fork in his direction. "So you mean you like bedding me and dining with me?"

Brett shrugged. "Well, when you put it like that…"

She grinned and settled back against the pillows to devour her fruit, before reaching for the coffee and muffin he'd brought for her.

"So we still on to meet Logan today?" she asked.

Brett wished they could have just stayed in their nice little bubble without involving Logan, but he knew there was little he could do to get out of it now. Trouble was, it wasn't so much how Logan would react that was troubling him, it was that he knew what he would say. And Brett knew that every word that came out of his friend's mouth would be the truth, exactly what he'd already struggled with, and he didn't want to second-guess what he was doing with Jamie when it already felt so fragile.

"How about we finish breakfast, you get yourself ready, then we take a walk before we meet him."

Jamie took a sip of her coffee. "Deal."

Jamie looked at Brett. He was staring into the distance.

"Everything okay?" she asked.

He turned to meet her gaze and smiled, but she could tell he had something on his mind. The kiss he dropped to her lips told her the problem wasn't her, but she still wanted to know. She was pleased they'd decided to walk Bear before meeting Logan for lunch—it gave them time to relax and just enjoy being together.

"It's Logan, isn't it? You're worried about telling him," Jamie stated as soon as he pulled away.

"It's not that I don't want to tell him, I can just see how this is going to go," he said, his hand stroking her hair as he looked into her eyes. "Part of me thinks we should just pretend like everything is normal, then go back to this when we return to your place."

Jamie sighed. On some level she agreed with him, but she didn't want to lie to Logan, and she didn't believe he was going to take it that badly. Not if they were honest about how everything had happened between them, that it wasn't something they'd ever have acted upon if the circumstances had been different.

"Let's just see how it goes. Maybe we're overthinking it."

He didn't look like he agreed, but he took her hand and tugged her in the direction they needed to head in. "For my sake, I hope you're right."

"Your sake?" she queried.

"Yeah, my sake. Because he'll never believe you could do any wrong, which means that I'll be the villain. He'll hate me and he'll feel sorry for you."

Jamie hoped he was being dramatic, even as her heart started to race at the thought of things going bad. Was she being naive to think Logan would behave like an adult and hear them out?

"Come on, Bear. Let's go," she ordered, giving him a hand signal to run on ahead. He bounded off, cheerful and content, just like she'd been before they'd started talking about Logan.

"Why don't you take my mind off everything by telling me about your book project," he said.

Jamie giggled. "I thought you were going to suggest something else entirely."

He pretended to look horrified. "We're in the middle of a public park, Jamie. Shame on you."

She just kept laughing and he wrapped his arm around her so she could loop hers around his waist. "I'm writing about happy things. Fairies and flying ponies, and little girls who can achieve whatever they dream."

"Sounds good."

"I just wanted to write about a fun little world that was a happy place. So I could escape each time I sat down at the computer or sketched the illustrations. Although I can't say the topic of the book has compelled me to work on it for any decent stretch of time."

"There's nothing wrong with wanting to escape reality," Brett told her, kissing the top of her head when she leaned her cheek against his shoulder. "We all have to do what we have to do."

"Which is why you didn't want to tell Logan," she remarked.

"Look, we can deal with Logan. Let's just not let it ruin this, okay?"

"I couldn't have said it better myself," she said. Because she had no intention of letting anyone or anything ruin what was happening between them.

Jamie stood up when she saw Logan enter the restaurant. They were sitting outside so Bear could be with them, and she didn't think he'd see them. Brett hadn't bothered to stand—he seemed more interested in shredding his sugar packet into a thousand pieces than looking out for his friend.

"Hey!" she called out when she spotted Logan.

He wrapped her in a big bear hug, holding on tight. "We don't see each other in months and now twice in a week. How lucky am I?"

She gave him a kiss on the cheek and stood back as Brett rose and the boys did some handshake-backslap ritual.

"You two hanging out a bit?" Logan asked.

Brett cleared his throat and she jumped in to answer for him. She'd hoped for a relaxed coffee first, that they could just hang out and enjoy catching up, but it seemed they were diving straight into it.

"Brett's actually staying with me, keeping me company," she said. "It's nice to have someone in the house again."

"Oh, yeah?" Logan answered, waving over a waitress and ordering a latte before picking up the menu.

"So you've been working? How's your

dog?" Brett asked. "Jamie's doing really well with Bear."

Jamie frowned at him, not wanting to change the subject yet. She just wanted to get everything out on the table, deal with the two most important men in her life by being honest. Then they could get back to chitchat and food, but they needed to get this out in the open now, especially since they were already on the topic.

"We should let the dogs get together for a play, take them to the beach or something," Logan said, before turning to Brett. "And you can stay with me if you need a place to crash once Jamie kicks you out, because we both know she'll be sick of you soon, right?"

Both guys laughed, but she didn't. Jamie tapped her fingers on the tabletop, trying to figure out how to get what she needed to say out there without Logan completely losing the plot.

"I thought you'd be staying at the barracks?" Brett asked.

"I've rented a place not far from there, and no one seems to mind me living offsite. They're putting me on some local work, security and bomb checks for the celebrities they have coming in over the next few months as part of the Visit Australia tourism campaign."

"Logan, there's something we need to tell you," Jamie blurted, interrupting their talk about Logan's work. It wasn't that she wasn't interested in what he was saying, about what he did, but she couldn't sit here pretending like they didn't have something major to discuss with him.

He put down his menu, looked from her to Brett and back to her again. "Is everything okay? It's not Bear, is it?" he asked, diverting his gaze to study the dog sitting at her feet, before reaching down to pat him. "You look good, boy. Jamie looking after you, huh?"

"We didn't mean for this to happen, especially not so soon after Sam passing away, but Brett and I are, well, we're close. We're, um, well we've become more than friends, and we wanted you to be the first to know." Damn it! That hadn't come out well at all, not as she'd planned, not like she'd practiced in her head. She didn't want to stuff this conversation up, and that was exactly what she'd managed to do.

Logan's fists had clenched on the table and she could see a tick at his temple.

"Logan, I can explain…" Brett began, before Logan cut him off straight away.

"Our friend dies, and instead of looking after his wife, *like we both promised to do,* you decide it's okay to sleep with her? To just slot into Sam's life like you can take his place?"

"It wasn't like that," Jamie told him, reaching for Brett's hand. "This wasn't planned, it's just…"

"So you *are* sleeping together?" he demanded.

"Logan, I can explain," she stuttered, emotion clogging her throat and making it near impossible to speak.

"Jamie, this is between me and Brett. You're a widow and we promised Sam we'd look after you, and instead he's has taken advantage of you?"

Her hands were wet, clammy from the tension at her table, and she was starting to flush hot. *This was not good.* There was no part of this that was good. Brett had been right, they should never have told Logan, they should have just stayed in their own little bubble of happiness.

"Logan, I didn't want to tell you, but we…"

Logan laughed, but it was a harsh sound that made Jamie cringe. "Please don't insult me or Sam by using the word *we* when it comes to Jamie, Brett."

Jamie didn't know what to say, hated that they were starting to have a conversation about her as if she weren't present, as if she couldn't hear every single word they were saying. She'd known pain, plenty of it lately, but this cut straight to the bone.

"Logan, why don't we go and talk about this somewhere private?" Brett asked. "Leave Jamie out of this."

"Oh, I have every intention of leaving her out of this," he said, seething.

Jamie watched as they both stood. They were big men, tall and muscled, and the testosterone surrounding her was enough to make her head spin. She knew this wasn't looking good, that at least one of them was about to explode, but she'd never seen either of them be violent before. Surely they wouldn't…

Jamie's mouth went dry. She swiveled in

her chair to watch them as they walked down the steps. It seemed too calm, too orderly, but the heated exchange that began when they were on the footpath was anything other than calm, and deep down she'd known it was coming. As soon as she'd seen Logan's expression, when she'd told him, she'd known. Her hand dropped to Bear, kneading his fur as she stayed seated.

Logan was in Brett's face, and he wasn't doing anything to stop him. Until he said one sentence. One sentence that Jamie heard even from where she was sitting, her hand now resting on Bear's head as she stared at the pair of them arguing. Her heart was thumping so hard she could hardly concentrate, a ringing in her ears making her head pound.

"I love her, Logan."

She froze, her hand stopping its back-and-forth stroke of her dog's head. There was nothing that could have prepared her for that moment, the second that she heard Brett say those three little words that sent her mind spiraling, that made it almost impossible for her to breathe.

He loved her.

Only the moment was shattered by the crack of Logan's fist hitting Brett square in the jaw. Jamie screamed, or at least she thought it was her because all she could hear was the ringing of a scream in her ears as she watched Brett stagger backward and Logan stand there, staring down at him, disgust written all over his face. Brett stood, not moving even as Logan raised his fist again, obviously deciding he wasn't going to engage, that he didn't want to fight his friend. In less than a minute, Logan stormed off down the footpath without a backward glance, disappearing before she even thought to call out to him. Before she was even capable of acting. Before she could do anything to right the wrong that had just happened because of her. Because she was as much in shock from what Brett had said, not just because of what Logan had done.

She flew down the steps and reached for Brett, gasping at the blood pouring from his nose and dripping into his mouth.

"Brett? Oh, my gosh…" The words came out like they were all connected, a complete jumble. "I don't, are you…?"

This couldn't be happening. Her hands were fluttering in the air with no idea what they should be doing to help him. And she still couldn't stop thinking about how it had felt to hear those words—*he loved her*.

"I'm fine," he insisted, wiping at his face then cursing when he covered his shirtsleeve in blood.

"No, you're not fine," she managed to say. "I'll cancel our lunch and then we can…"

"No," he said, staring down at her with a coolness in his gaze that sent shivers down her spine. This was not the same man she'd made love to, the same man whose hand she'd held as they strolled through the park earlier. The man who'd just confessed his love for her. "There can be no *us*, Jamie, don't you get that now? This is why I didn't want to meet Logan, because I knew that he'd tell me what I already knew, what I've been trying to ignore this whole time."

She stood dead-still, feet rooted to the spot, unable to move even if she wanted to. "Just because Logan didn't understand doesn't mean this is wrong. He'll get his head around it, eventually. We knew this wasn't going to be easy for him to digest, Brett, we knew it was going to be tough."

"It's not about Logan accepting us or not, Jamie, it's about him being *right*. Maybe this is me taking advantage of you, doing something that is so wrong it shouldn't have even crossed my mind that any part of it was okay." He stared at her. "Sam was my best friend, Jamie, and he trusted me like he trusted no one else. Except for Logan. And now I've lost both of them, because I did something that I've known was wrong every step of the way." He stared at her, his expression empty. "It doesn't matter how I feel about you, Jamie. I should never have let this go so far between us. I shouldn't have told you about looking for you, about seeing Sam with you. None of it."

Jamie stared back up at him, digging her fingernails into her palm, determined to stay strong.

"So what are you saying, Brett?"

He looked at her then looked away, like he couldn't even make eye contact with her anymore. "I need to think," he said, walking a few steps backward, putting enough space between them that it felt like they'd never be close, that he'd never hold her in his arms or kiss her ever again. "I'll see you later."

Jamie stood and watched him—the man she'd just opened herself up to, the man who'd only moments earlier said he loved her—walk away. Instead of fighting for her, fighting for their right to be together, he'd just given up and left her. And she had a feeling that he wasn't just walking away from lunch, he was walking away from *her. For good.*

She squared her shoulders and forced herself to walk back up the steps and into the restaurant, hating that the other people seated outside in the courtyard had witnessed the scene and no doubt heard some of what was being said. Bear's wagging tail made her smile, though, and she dropped a kiss to his head before sitting back down again, trying to stay calm. Her dog was at least loyal, would never leave her side unless she wanted him to. Bear was the only constant in her life right now, no strings attached.

"Ma'am, would you like to cancel one of your orders?"

She nodded bravely. "Yes, just the eggs

benedict for me, please. And another latte. Make it strong."

There was a newspaper at the empty table beside her, so she reached for it and started scanning the articles. She wasn't interested in reading, but she was interested in doing anything she could to take her mind off Brett. To try to keep things normal and pretend that everything was okay for a little while.

If that meant sitting alone with her dog to eat brunch, then that's what she'd do. She needed to be grateful for her life, for the fact that she was sitting here, alive, in the sun. She could go home and cry later, but right now she was going to eat her eggs and drink her coffee.

Because she'd put herself through enough, *been* through enough, to just take a moment for herself and pretend like everything was okay. Inside, she wanted to fall apart, but her mind was strong, and she wanted to keep it that way. Life didn't get much tougher than losing a husband, but she'd survived that, and she would survive this. Just like she'd survived losing her dad when she was a teenager and dealt with a mom who'd been more interested in drowning her sorrows in a bottle of wine than comforting her only daughter.

She was a fighter, and she wasn't going to lose her strength, not ever.

CHAPTER TWELVE

JAMIE WAS TIRED. She was tired of waiting, tired of thinking, tired of everything. She'd read through the final draft of her latest manuscript, played around with all of her sketches to send her editor, but nothing was inspiring her. And now here she was, curled up in her favorite chair again with a cup of coffee, staring out the window. She'd spent a lot of time sitting in the same spot and thinking after Sam had died, after the men had come knocking at her door and told her the news, and it was the only place she felt like sitting now. She didn't know why, but whenever she looked out the window it helped her to relax.

Bear's low whine broke her trance, and she smiled over at him. He'd been through so much, which made them perfect companions, but she also knew that the only reason she was doing so well with the dog now was because of Brett.

Brett. She couldn't stop thinking about him if she tried. He was the only person who'd made her feel alive, who'd made her feel like *her* again since Sam had died, and now he'd gone and walked away. Not to mention the wedge she'd driven between him and Logan—a wedge she was worried might be irreparable.

I love her. They were the words that had echoed in her head since the fight. Maybe she'd heard them wrong, maybe he'd said something else, but the way her heart picked up speed whenever she played that moment over in her mind told her that she'd been right. That there was no mistaking what he'd told Logan, before she'd heard the smack of Logan's fist against his face. How could he feel that way about her and still walk away?

It excited and terrified her in equal parts, because this was Brett. Her friend, Brett. Her husband's friend, Brett. And he was also the man she'd made love to the night before and couldn't stop thinking about. The only man other than her husband who she could ever imagine being with, and the only man she wanted to be with. But now he was gone, and she'd never have the chance to hear the words from his lips, or say them back to him.

Jamie sighed again and reached for her phone, checking to make sure she hadn't missed a call or a text. Eventually she was going to have to admit that Brett wasn't coming back, at least not tonight. She was alone, again. Just her and Bear, and what she'd shared with Brett might be over for good, just a memory.

"Want a cuddle?" she asked the dog. She moved to the sofa and grabbed a blanket to tuck around herself.

He pricked his ears and watched as she settled herself, flicked on the television and patted the spot beside her. It didn't take him long to decide to join her—he padded over and jumped up, taking up more space than she was. But she didn't care. He was a warm body and he loved her, and that was all she needed right now. Bear was her oversized cuddly blanket—not to mention her protector at night.

Her dog was someone who wasn't going to leave her, someone who was supposed to

be by her side, no questions asked. Someone who'd be in her life for as long as was
possible.

Someone she could love without feeling
guilty about what her heart was telling her.

Brett leaned both elbows on the counter and
stared down into his drink. The warm brown
liquid didn't have any answers, and it wasn't
a vice he'd ever indulged before, but after
what had happened with Jamie, he'd decided
a bourbon might help clear his head. Not that
it was doing the pounding any good, or helping the purple swirl that was starting around
his eye and across one side of his nose. He'd
taken one look in the cracked bathroom mirror and decided that he was best not to look
at the reminder on his face.

He held up the glass and took a small sip,
cringing as the liquid burned a fiery trail
down his throat. It was only early afternoon,
and he never drank straight spirits at the best
of times, let alone on an empty stomach.

Brett glanced around at the other people in
the bar—all men. It was dark and dingy, an
underground dive that made it almost impossible to remember that it was a bright, sunny

day outside. The kind of day he should be enjoying, rather than sitting around feeling sorry for himself.

He swallowed a larger gulp of his drink this time, finding the second taste smoother than the first.

"You ready for another?"

Brett looked up as the bartender spoke to him. "Ah, no. I think just one will do me."

He received a nod in response. "I haven't seen you here before."

"And hopefully, at this time of the day at least, you won't see me again."

The bartender chuckled. "You don't exactly look like my kind of lunchtime regular. The type who only ever consumes liquid for lunch, that is."

"Heaven help me," Brett said, tipping back the rest of the glass and closing his eyes as he swallowed it down. The drink had made his stomach swirl with a heat that felt better than the cold dread he'd been experiencing earlier, but he still didn't want to be tempted by a second.

"Woman trouble?"

Brett nodded. "You could say that."

"Don't be an idiot, that's my advice. If you

love her? Tell her you're sorry and make it up to her. The guys that don't do that…?" The bartender raised his eyebrows. "They're the ones who turn into my regulars, and it's a sad story from then on. Although women troubles are pretty good for business down here."

Brett stood and put his wallet into his back pocket. "Thanks for the advice. It's not quite that simple, but you're right."

He walked to the entrance, feeling like a desperate man as he stared at the light filtering through the door. Suddenly the confines of the bar, the darkness, even the smell, were all telling him that he needed to run, and fast. Before he turned into a depressed creature who needed bourbon and darkness to deal with his life on a daily basis.

Brett's memories would forever haunt him—that last day with Sam like a scene from a movie playing on repeat sometimes— but he wasn't ever going to give in to them. He had been part of Australia's most elite special forces team, was trained in active combat, even how to deal with being captured and held by an enemy, and that training had instilled a strength in him that he wasn't ever going to let disappear from his mind.

The trouble was, that training had also taught him that there was nothing more important than his fellow soldiers, *his men*. And Sam had been his wingman, his buddy, the person he trusted with his life on a daily basis. Part of the family that he'd created after losing his parents.

So did he maintain that loyalty even in Sam's death, or did he give in to his feelings for Jamie and try to tell himself that *that* was the right thing to do? Because the broken, hurt look in her eyes when he'd walked away from her earlier might end up haunting him for the rest of his life, too. He loved her, there was no denying that, but he also had a loyalty to his family, and that meant respecting Sam even in death. What Logan had said was what had terrified him all this time with Jamie—words that he'd told himself before giving in to the way he felt. Before making love to Jamie and knowing it was so wrong, but also so right.

Brett held up his hand to shield his eyes from the bright sunlight and started to walk, because he had nothing else to do and nowhere else to be. He just followed his feet, needing the time to think. He hadn't been lying to Jamie when he'd told her how he'd felt that first time they'd met, or about how he'd come looking for her, and part of him knew that she deserved to know the truth about the past. About how he'd felt and what he would have done if she hadn't already met Sam.

That night, that first time they'd met, they'd spent hours talking. Two people at a party, not part of the crowd around them, they'd sipped champagne, laughed and talked like he'd never talked to anyone in his life before. And then his girlfriend had interrupted them, told him off for leaving her even though he'd seen her dancing and having fun without him, knew she'd been fine on her own.

He'd walked away from Jamie, tugged in a direction that he'd known had been wrong, but knowing that he didn't have a choice. The look in her eyes, the way they'd looked at one another, was a moment he'd never forgotten. His hand held by one woman, and everything else held by a woman he'd only known for less than a few hours.

Ten minutes later, from across the room, he'd watched her leave, and the next time he'd seen her, she'd been laughing and in the arms of his best friend. *Sam*.

Brett stopped walking and stared up at the sky, eyes adjusted to the sun now

He'd fallen in love with Jamie from the moment he'd met her. So what if it wasn't the right thing in everyone else's eyes? If it wasn't what he'd planned? He'd stood back and let his friend be with the love of his life, and now it was his turn, wasn't it? It was his chance at a happiness that he'd never known, his time to see if he and Jamie could be together. Did it mean he didn't love Sam like a brother, now that Sam was gone and he and Jamie had the chance to fall in love?

If Jamie wanted him, then he was a fool to walk away, he knew that. Logan might be his friend, but Jamie could be the love of his life, the woman who'd be at his side for the rest of his life. And that wasn't something anyone else had the right to tell him he should give up. Not Logan, and not Sam's memory. Because no matter how much he respected his friends, he needed to respect himself and what was important to him, too.

If they were truly his family, wouldn't they want to see him happy?

The only person who had the right to push him away and end whatever it was that had happened between them, was Jamie. He just needed to tell her that before she changed her mind and didn't want him back.

He'd spent so long worrying about what other people would think was right, about being faithful to those he loved, that he'd forgotten what was most important. What was right by Jamie. What would make Jamie happy.

What would make him happy.

And there was only one thing that could make him happy right now, and that was Jamie, in his life, in his arms.

He wanted to give her enough time to think, to deal with what had happened, but he didn't want to leave it so long that she thought he didn't care.

Brett headed toward a café he could see across the street and decided to have a late lunch, just sit for a while and eat, think about what he'd say to her. Because this could be the most important thing he ever prepared for in his life, and he didn't want to screw up the one chance he might get to prove himself to Jamie.

CHAPTER THIRTEEN

BRETT CROSSED THE street and looked at Jamie's house. It was like the first day he'd arrived, when he'd been so uncertain about coming, about what he'd say to her, and now he was feeling just as awkward.

Only this time, he actually had something to be awkward about. Not to mention something to say that he couldn't even rehearse right in his mind, let alone out loud in front of Jamie.

It was getting late but the streetlights raised the canopy of darkness. She would no doubt already be asleep, but he was ready to come back and if he didn't do it now he might never do it. He'd needed to take his time, to think and be sure about the decision he'd made, and now there was no doubt in his mind that what he was about to do was right.

Brett slid his key into the lock and turned it, quietly opening the door and shutting it behind him. Jamie had given him the key, willingly invited him into her home, but he still felt weird about just letting himself in and treating it like his own place. Especially after what had happened. She'd probably hear him and think he was an intruder, not expecting him to ever show his face again, and the last thing he wanted was to fuel her memories of what had happened in her childhood home.

"Just me, Bear," he called out in a low voice, not wanting the dog to attack him thinking he was a stranger.

He walked through the house, flicked the light on in the kitchen, and it was then he heard the low growl. Brett looked around and realized the noise was coming from the sofa.

"Hey, boy, just me. It's Brett," he whispered.

The growl turned to a whine, and he stepped toward him so Bear could see him. His eyes adjusted to the half-light and he saw that the dog was snuggled up to, and protecting, Jamie. She was sound asleep, head tucked into a large cushion, blanket half over her, half over Bear. He knew better than to approach him too quickly.

Brett didn't want to wake Jamie and give her a fright, either, so he quietly moved toward the sofa, pulled the blanket up to her chin without disturbing her or the dog, then walked back to turn the kitchen light off. He made his way in the dark into the living room again and slumped down in the armchair. It wasn't the most comfortable place to sleep, but he'd experienced far worse, and he wanted to be there when Jamie woke up.

He didn't want her to think he'd spent the night somewhere else, wanted her to know that he cared enough to come home and deal with what a jerk he'd been earlier in the day. And most of all, he wanted to be near her. This last week had made him feel alive again—being around Jamie and Bear—and he wasn't going to give that up without a fight. Not to mention the fact that he'd finally been able to sleep since he'd been in her home with her. And if she asked him to leave in the morning? At least he could tell himself that he'd tried, that it wasn't his own fear than had driven a wedge between them. He'd respect her choice no matter what she decided.

Brett was starting to be thankful that he'd had the glass of bourbon, because without it, he may have ended up sitting awake all night. But the heaviness in his eyes told him he needed to sleep, and he wasn't going to deny himself. Not with Jamie asleep on the sofa opposite him. There was nothing he could do until she woke up, which gave him a little longer before he had to pour his heart out and convince her that what he'd said earlier, the way he'd behaved, had been him acting way out of line.

The truth had been how he'd held her in his arms the night before, what he'd said to her these past few days. Today, he'd just been plain scared, and that wasn't something he would ever have admitted to in the past.

Jamie woke to the sun shining on her face and a big body pinning her down. She could hardly feel her legs. When she opened her eyes it was to a large black nose, with Bear resting his head on her chest.

"You're squashing me," she muttered,

pushing the hair from her face, trying again to stretch out her legs and failing. He either didn't hear her, or didn't care, because he didn't budge an inch and she was suddenly claustrophobic.

"Morning."

Jamie's heart stuttered into a superfast beat. Brett? What was he doing here? She locked eyes on him.

"When did you get back?" She hadn't been expecting him here, let alone waking to find him in the same room as her.

"Ah, last night. But you looked so comfortable on the sofa so I left you there. Sorry if I woke you."

She pushed Bear off and stretched, making an attempt to push her hair down, knowing how terrible she must look. She'd curled up without washing any of her makeup off, so her hair was probably the least of her worries compared to her panda eyes.

"You don't have to make breakfast," she told him, standing to watch Brett as he moved around the kitchen.

His dark brown eyes met hers, and she couldn't help but smile at him. *This was Brett.* No matter what had happened yesterday, he was still the same Brett she'd always loved as a friend, and now…what? She didn't know how to describe what had happened between them, how she felt about this gorgeous, kind man cooking in her kitchen. But she did know that she didn't want to lose him from her life.

"I want to make up for yesterday's lunch disaster," he told her, cracking eggs into the pan as he spoke. "I know it's going to take more than eggs to apologize, but it's a good start, right?"

Jamie nodded, smiling back at him, but she needed a moment to gather her thoughts, to be alone. To deal with the fact that she'd gone to bed thinking she might never hear from him again, and now she was about to sit down to breakfast with him. Thank God she hadn't woken in the night and tried to attack him, thinking he was breaking in.

"I'm just going to freshen up. I won't be long," she told him.

Jamie headed for the bathroom and shut the door behind her. What she wanted to do was sink to the floor and feel the cool of the tiles against her skin, but she also wanted to hear what Brett had to say. He was either going to tell her he wanted to go back to just being friends, or that he wanted something more, and she needed to prepare herself either way. She wanted him here so badly, but she also had no intention of forcing him.

Not to mention she was terrified of losing him as a friend.

Brett had been trying to rehearse what he was going to say, but the trouble was that he wasn't entirely sure *what* he wanted to tell her. He put the eggs and bacon on the plates and walked them to the table, before returning with the toast and then the pot of coffee he'd freshly brewed. They said food was the way to a man's heart—he was the hoping the same might be true for women. Or just one woman in particular.

"It looks great."

He looked up as Jamie entered the room, watching as she first looked down at the table, then at him, before sitting. She immediately fingered the napkin he'd put beside her plate, as if she needed something to do, something to take her mind off what was happening or what they were going to talk about.

"The scrambled eggs look so creamy," she said, taking a mouthful and fluttering her eyes shut for a second as she swallowed. "And they taste *really* good."

"The trick is to not add any milk. Just whisk them all up and straight into the pan, and turn them off as soon as they're almost cooked."

"So you know more than just pasta and sauce, huh? What happened to you being a one-trick pony?"

Brett swallowed his mouthful and reached for a piece of toast. "One breakfast recipe and one dinner, that's all." He took a bite and watched her. "Now that you've tasted this, I don't have any more hidden talents to wow you with. This is me going all out to impress."

Jamie smiled, but before she could reply he cleared his throat.

"I didn't cook you breakfast to brag about my skills in the kitchen, Jamie. I wanted to say sorry. To genuinely tell you how sorry I am for what happened and for what I said. I was a jerk and I never should have behaved like that."

She shook her head. "You don't need to

apologize. I should never have insisted we tell Logan, not so soon. It was stupid and I have no idea what I was thinking."

Brett put down his fork and leaned toward her, both arms on the table. "If we hadn't told him we would have been lying, and telling him later would have been worse. He would have felt betrayed, so you were right. I just wish it had happened differently, and if I could do anything to change that, I would."

"So what are you trying to tell me?" she asked, picking at small bits of egg as she glanced up at him.

"What I'm trying to say is that no matter how badly it went down yesterday, telling Logan was the right thing. He's been with me, with us all, through thick and thin, and I don't want to lose him. The way I reacted was unacceptable, but everything he said just kind of fueled what I'd been worried about all along."

Jamie was looking at her food, eating little mouthfuls like she wasn't really hungry, but he waited her out, knowing she'd look up eventually. What he hadn't said was that he didn't want to lose her, either, but right now he wasn't even sure she was his to lose.

He picked up a piece of bacon between his fingers and crunched on it, never taking his eyes from her, and when she looked up he was ready. Or at least he was ready for the connection. What he wasn't ready for was the bright blue of her irises, the way they looked as if they were bathed in water from the tears glistening in them, the sight of her bottom lip tucked under her teeth, like she was having to bite on it to stop from crying—it was almost enough to break his heart.

"Why did you come back last night, Brett? Was it just to tell me that, or something more?"

Brett put the piece of bacon down that he'd been holding and wiped his fingers on his napkin. This was his moment, this was the chance he'd been waiting for, and he wasn't going to blow it.

"I came back because I was a coward yesterday, and that's not the man I am."

"I know you're no coward," she told him, a smile curving her lips and taking the sadness from her face. "You're one of the bravest people I know, and the fact that you didn't punch Logan back, and that you walked away from me? Neither of those things makes you a coward, it just makes you a person who doesn't want to do the wrong thing by the people you care about."

"I deserved the bloody nose, it's not that, but walking away from you?" He shook his head. "That was the worst decision I've ever made in my life, and I need you to know that I will never walk away from you like that ever again. I was stupid to let fear stop me from doing the one thing in my life that I've never been so sure about. *How I feel about you.*"

Brett's voice was husky, a deeper tone than it usually was. He pushed his chair out and moved around to Jamie, taking her hands in his and dropping to his knees beside her instead of towering over her.

"You're the best thing that has ever happened to me, Jamie," he told her, staring into her eyes. "What we did, what we're doing, it might not have been planned, but I'm going to fight for you if I have to. I don't care who says no and stands in our way, if you want me here, then I won't ever leave you. And that's a promise I will never break."

Jamie had tears falling down her cheeks now in a slow, steady stream. "I only want you here if you want to be here," she whispered. "I need to know how you feel about me."

She reached out and touched just under his eye, where he knew he was sporting a nasty black bruise. Her fingers were feather-light, tracing across his skin.

"I've never wanted anything so bad in all my life," he admitted. "Or any*one*."

"I can't lose another man I love, Brett. I can't…" The words were low, almost a whisper.

"I'll promise in front of every single person we know if I have to, to make you believe me, but I will never, *ever* let you down Jamie. I'm here for you, for as long as you'll have me. You're my family, too, not just the guys."

Her fingers traced beneath his bruise again before reaching around to his ear, then to the back of his head. She pulled him toward her and leaned close, her face only inches from his.

"I think I love you, Brett," she whispered, tilting her mouth toward him, lips parted.

He didn't hesitate. Brett closed his mouth over hers, lips crushed to Jamie's and moving just enough, drinking in the taste of her, the warmth of having her body and mouth pressed to his.

He only pulled back because he had to, because he needed to tell her how he felt, too.

"I don't *think* I love you, Jamie," he whispered, mouth hovering so close to hers as he spoke that her plump lips just touched his. *"I know so."*

Jamie held on to the back of Brett's head, drawing him back to her again, her mouth taking his captive. He wasn't going to stop her, but he did want to make things more comfortable.

He dragged her hand from his hair, lips barely leaving hers, and slowly moved them down to the carpet, tugging her down on top of him.

"Sorry about breakfast," she whispered, as she put her hands on either side of his head to brace herself.

"Screw breakfast," he muttered as he flipped her on to her back, so he was braced above her. "I'll take you over food any day."

"Oh, yeah?" Her fingers grabbed hold of a fistful of his hair.

"Yeah."

Brett tried to growl but she just laughed at him and tugged him lower.

"Shut up and kiss me," she said.

"Yes, ma'am."

She laughed as he kissed the hollow of her neck, just above her collarbone, holding down her arms so she was powerless to move. His lips slowly moved up her neck, before settling on her mouth. His grip on her loosened as she submitted to his kiss, moaning as his tongue teased hers, lips soft one moment then rough.

Jamie pushed up his shirt, hands sliding against his bare skin, moving across his scars and up to his shoulders, then down again.

"That's a dangerous game you're playing," he muttered against her mouth.

"I know," she whispered back as she ran her hands up his stomach this time, taking her time so she could feel his muscles, exploring every inch of him.

"Do you want me to strip you naked here on the floor?"

Hmm. She did like the sound of that… "Is that a take-it-or-leave-it question?"

"No," he said, nose against hers as he stared into her eyes. "Multichoice."

She waited, his breath hot against her skin.

"The other option is that I pick you up and drag you to your bedroom. So I can have my wicked way with you there," he said, his voice deep and husky.

There was no mistaking what he wanted from her, and she wanted it every bit as bad.

"I'll take option two," she said, liking her newfound confidence, that she could tell him what she wanted without being too shy. "It just so happens that I have nothing else to do today, so my schedule's clear."

"So I'm just some toy to pass the time with?" he asked, holding her down by the wrists again and kissing her, before hauling her up and scooping her up into his arms.

Jamie slung her arms around his neck, loving that he was strong enough to just pick her up and carry her, like he was her protector. She knew she could take care of herself, but knowing she had a man in her life who'd stand by her side no matter what was something she loved.

"No, I'm saying you're my lover, and I want you to…" She didn't finish the sentence, the heat in his gaze making the words stall in her throat.

"Lover, huh?"

"Unless you don't want to be?" she asked, catching her bottom lip beneath her teeth.

"Oh, I want to be," he said, forcing her lips to his in a kiss that left her breathless. "Just don't expect me to let you out of your room anytime soon."

Jamie pressed her face into his chest as he carried her down the hall and kicked the bedroom door shut behind them.

Last night she'd been miserable, and this morning she was so happy she couldn't stop smiling.

Brett put her carefully on the bed and stared down at her. "I love you, Jamie," he said, all hint of playfulness gone, his tone serious. "I'm *in* love with you."

"I'm in love with you, too," she said back, not hesitating, loving that she was hearing the words straight from his mouth as he looked into her eyes, rather than second-hand, as he had admitted them to Logan.

Brett lowered himself over her and kissed her again, softer this time, more gently.

It was time for her to let go of the past and make a new future with this gorgeous, kind man, and there was no part of her that wasn't sure. She wanted to be with Brett, and no one was going to take that from her. Not ever.

Sunlight was pouring into the room, and Jamie was fighting to keep her eyes open.

"You know, I don't think I've ever been in bed at this time in the afternoon before," she mused.

Brett laughed, which sounded like a weird kind of rumbling from where she had her head pressed to his chest. She was curled up beside him, the sheet half-covering them, as she basked in the way he was stroking his fingers across her skin. Jamie felt like a well-petted cat, so content she could have purred, loving that he couldn't seem to take his hands off her.

"It feels good, doesn't it?"

"What?" she murmured. "You touching me like this? Because you can keep doing it until it's dark out, or forever, for that matter."

Brett moved his hand to stroke her hair. "Just being together. Not fighting it anymore."

"You know that Sam wouldn't have been angry with us," she said, wishing she didn't have to break the intimate moment between them, but needing to say what was on her mind. Jamie pushed up and stared down at Brett. "It doesn't mean I didn't love him with all my heart, but I think we met all those years ago for a reason, Brett. Because I met two men I could have fallen for, two men I might not have been able to decide between if I'd known that you'd come looking for me, and it's our time now. It's never been right before, but it is now."

Brett had an expression on his face that she couldn't read, but she could at least tell that he wasn't angry.

"I'm not scared of facing Sam one day," Brett told her, his lips kicking into a half smile. "He knows I would have traded places with him if I could have the day that bomb went off, and by the time I do see him, he'll be able to tell that I loved you just as much as he did."

Jamie dropped a slow, casual kiss to Brett's lips. "So are we just going to live in bliss for a while and never leave the house, take baby steps?"

Brett's face turned more somber and he sat up and propped himself against the pillows. "I know it didn't go well the first time, but I think we need to try to talk to Logan again."

Her eyebrows shot up. "You do?" The thought terrified her, especially how things had turned out, what she'd gone through thinking that Brett had left her.

He ran his fingers through her hair and tucked a few wisps behind her ear, his eyes never leaving hers. "Nothing is going to scare me off or change the way I feel about you Jamie, but Logan is important to both of us, and I want to try to make amends. Make him see that this is real, that this isn't something that's going to go away just because it makes him uncomfortable. I want to explain to him why everything he said is flawed, why this is right."

She nodded, sighing as his hand cupped her cheek and she relaxed into it. "Okay. I just don't want to burst this perfect little bubble we're floating in right now. I want to stay like this forever."

"We won't ruin this, not this time," he said. "I promise."

She trusted him, but she also knew how Logan's disapproval could affect them both if it went bad again. "So if he punches you again or tries to make us feel disgusting for what we've done?"

Brett leaned forward to drop a kiss to her forehead. "Then we tell him that his friendship means a lot to us, that he's family, but that we're in love and we need him to respect that. We're not going to change who we are or how we feel for anyone."

Jamie found herself nodding. "And when exactly are you proposing we do this?" she asked.

"Tomorrow."

"And everyone else in our lives?" she asked.

"We can take telling the rest of the world a little slower, I think," he said, pulling her closer so he could put his arms around her. "Logan can be our first step, and then we'll just take it one day at a time. Do what feels right, when it feels right."

Jamie shut her eyes and relaxed against Brett's bare chest, happy that it was warm enough that they could just lie naked, with only the light sheet covering them.

"You have a plan for how we convince him to see us again?"

He tightened his hold on her. "You can organize to meet him, say you want to talk with him, take the dogs to the river or something," Brett told her. "No matter how angry he is with me, he'll never say no to seeing you."

"You sure about that?" she mumbled against his chest.

"I'm sure," he said. "When I turn up, too, he'll have no choice other than to see me, to hear what I have to say."

"If that's how you want to do it, then that's how we'll do it."

"Good," Brett said, hands stroking her back and disappearing beneath the sheets, against her skin. "Because now that that's sorted, I want to forget about everything else for the rest of the day and just think about you."

"Oh, really?" She laughed, wriggling as he held her, teased her.

"Yes, really," he said, capturing her mouth in a kiss that made her turn into liquid against him. "And that's only the start of it."

CHAPTER FOURTEEN

JAMIE HAD A flutter in her stomach that wasn't doing anything to help her nerves. She opened the back door of her car and signaled for Bear to jump out, just like Brett had instructed her to do with him, and he obediently hopped out and waited beside her.

"Don't overthink this."

She stared at Brett over the top of the car, where he was leaning. "I'm starting to think this wasn't such a good idea, that's what I'm thinking. Why didn't we just tell him that you would be coming?"

Brett sighed and walked around the car to her, and pulled her into his arms. "Because he would have said no, and he would have been angry before he even arrived."

She held on tight to him before stepping out of his embrace and clipping on Bear's leash. "Come on then, let's go and get this over with."

"You'll be fine. Just be yourself, and I'll deal with Logan if things don't go as planned."

Jamie shut her eyes, took a deep breath, then walked off through the park and to the river where she'd organized to meet Logan. For all her talk originally about wanting to be honest, about wanting Logan to know, she wasn't feeling so confident anymore. She would do anything to protect her relationship with Brett, and this felt like doing the exact opposite of what she should be doing.

"Once bitten, twice shy," she muttered to herself.

She looked across at Bear, wondering why he'd stopped walking, why he had his head cocked to one side, watching her. Jamie dropped to her haunches to give him a cuddle.

"I'm sorry, boy. I keep forgetting that you're always trying to figure out what I'm saying." She unclipped his leash, knowing it was about time she trusted him. "Let's go find your friend, huh? Off you go," she instructed, flinging her arm out in the signal Brett had taught her.

Bear gave her a look, like he was making sure he'd understood her properly, before trotting off ahead. She might be feeling more confident as a dog owner, but her knees were positively knocking over the idea of seeing Logan.

"Jamie!"

She looked up and saw him, standing by the river, hand held up in the air. Bear paused, looked back at her, clearly asking if he was allowed to run over to the other dog.

"Go see," she told him, walking faster herself and watching as he bounded off to say hello.

It was now or never.

"Hey, Logan," she called out when she was near.

"Hey," he replied, closing the distance between them and kissing her on the cheek.

It didn't feel anywhere near as awkward as she'd been expecting, seeing him after what had happened, but she knew everything would change when Brett appeared.

They both watched the dogs sniffing and

playing, happily getting to know one another again.

"Do you think they remember each other?" she asked.

"Yeah," Logan said, jamming his hands into his pockets. "They've spent months at a time in the same place, and I don't think they forget. They probably have better memories that we do."

"Want to take them for a wander?"

Logan nodded and gave the dogs a whistle. "Jamie, about what happened…"

"Logan, I don't want you to apologize. There was nothing about the other day that went as planned." Jamie touched her hand to his shoulder, squeezing slightly. "I'm sorry I put you in that position. It was wrong and we should have thought it through better instead of just springing the news on you."

He stopped and stared at her, like he wasn't sure what to say.

"You're going to hate me for saying this, but Brett? He deserved a black eye. I'm only sorry about the way I spoke to you."

She sighed, shaking her head. "But that's it, Logan. Brett didn't deserve it. I'm as much to blame as he is for what's happened between us. You can't not attribute some of your anger toward me."

"Jamie, sweetheart, you're a widow. You're probably lonely." His expression was kind but it also annoyed her, like the fact she'd lost her husband meant she couldn't make up her own mind about how she felt or what she did. "Brett took advantage of you, so it is his fault."

She knew she had to tell Logan the truth, now, before Brett turned up, because this conversation wasn't exactly going as planned. "Logan, Brett and I met before I even knew Sam. Pretending like us being together isn't partly my fault is just patronizing."

His eyebrows shot up and his face seemed to visibly harden. "I'm not sure I'm following you."

"Do you remember, years back, Brett telling you about a girl he'd met? A girl he spent weeks looking for?"

Logan laughed. "Yeah, and he never found her."

"But he did," she told him, voice low. "That girl was me, and I'd just started seeing Sam when Brett finally tracked me down."

"You two weren't…"

"No!" Jamie said, not wanting him to imagine the situation being worse than it was. "I remembered him, of course I remembered him, but he never said anything about looking for me, about the night we'd met. Because he could see how happy Sam was, and he took the high road and walked away. Until recently, he never even told me what had happened."

Logan shook his head. "I think we need to keep walking."

Jamie fell into step beside him, wanting desperately for him to understand what she was trying to say.

"Brett and I have always had feelings for each other, but nothing would ever have happened while I was married to Sam." She took another deep breath. "I loved Sam so much, and nothing could have jeopardized our marriage, but with him gone and Brett back?"

Logan didn't say anything, but she knew he was listening.

"The fact that something has happened between us now is okay, Logan, because we've done nothing wrong."

"Sam has only been gone…" He shrugged.

"Whatever I say isn't going to make a difference, is it? You've clearly already made up your mind."

Jamie slowly shook her head, but she panicked when she saw Brett walking in their direction.

"What?" Logan asked, looking over his shoulder. "What the hell is he doing here?"

"Don't overreact, he wanted to come and make things right with you."

"I should just leave," he muttered.

Jamie looped her arm through Logan's to keep him in place. "No, you're not. Because we're all adults here, and you guys are best mates. You're not falling out because of me, and you need to promise me that you'll listen to what he has to say."

She watched as the dogs ran over to Brett, running circles around him then bounding back off to the river to inspect the ducks again.

"Hey," Brett called out.

Logan stiffened, but she didn't let him go.

"Geez, your eye really came up," Logan said.

Brett shrugged. "Guess I deserved it." He passed them each a coffee from the cardboard tray he was holding. "I just want this coffee to go better than our last attempt, so can we all keep our fists to ourselves?"

Brett had angled his body slightly to watch the dogs, and Jamie knew Logan was watching him.

"You must miss Ted even more when you're around these two," Logan said.

Brett's eyes were nothing short of honest when he turned back, the look in them enough to break Jamie's heart. "It's easy for someone else to tell me he was just a dog, but I miss him like hell. All the time. I don't think I'll ever stop thinking about the way he died, about what I lost that day."

They all stood and sipped their coffee.

"Jamie told me, about her being the girl from all those years back."

Brett took another sip of his coffee before sending a smile in her direction. "I need you to know that I would never have come between Jamie and Sam, but I love her, Logan. I always have. This isn't something new for me, it's just something I've never acted on before."

Jamie could hardly breathe, she was terrified of what was going to happen now. Of what Logan was going to say. How his re-action could change everything.

"Did you come here wanting my blessing, or do you not care either way?" Logan asked.

"If I didn't care, I wouldn't have told you the other day, and I wouldn't be standing here now," Brett told him. "I'm not going to walk away from Jamie, but then I'm not planning on walking away from you, either. Not after all we've been through. I just want you to try to understand."

Logan started to walk, slowly, and they both started to move, too. The dogs were having a ball and they followed them along the gentle curve of the river.

"I think I just need some time to get my head around all this," Logan confessed, run-ning a hand through his short hair. "It's not that I want to be the one that comes between you two, I just need to process it. It's a lot to take in."

Jamie couldn't help the smile the spread across her face, and the wink Brett gave her made her heart race. It was a baby step, but it was a step in the right direction.

"You both mean too much to me to lose

either of you. So if you need time?" she said. "Take as much as you need."

"And you really think Sam would have been okay with this? That he wouldn't want me to do everything and anything to protect you? To stop you from making a mistake?"

"Logan, you don't need to protect her, because I'm not going to hurt her," Brett said, stopping at the same time Logan did. "Me walking away? That's what would hurt Jamie. And I love her." He smiled at her, eyes connecting with hers. "I love her, man."

Logan tipped his head back, eyes closed, before shaking his head and looking first at Jamie and then at Brett. "Just give me time. I just need time to wrap my head around all this."

Jamie knew when to change the subject, and that time was now. They'd told Logan what they needed to tell him, and it had gone down without anyone having their teeth knocked out, so now they just needed to hang out.

"Want to let the dogs have a swim?" she asked.

Logan laughed. "You ever had Bear in your car, soaking wet?"

Brett was laughing, too, and she couldn't not join in. "A quick swim and then a long walk so they can dry off, then," she suggested.

The guys exchanged looks and kept laughing, even as she told Bear to jump in and he did so with a massive bound, like he was a professional lifesaver. Ranger was barking on the sidelines, glancing back at Logan, waiting for the command. When he got it, he launched into the water, too, both dogs swimming toward a group of ducks.

"What's so funny?" she asked.

Brett's cheeky smile made her glare at him. "You. For thinking for a moment that you'll ever get your dog out of the water."

"What do you mean? He's so obedient." she said, annoyed with the way they were both grinning at her. "You told me he'll obey me at all times, Brett. Was there something you neglected to tell me?"

"Even Sam couldn't ever convince that dog to get out of the water. You? Not a chance."

Jamie threw her hands up in the air. "Maybe you could have told me that *before* he showed off his dive?"

"Nah, this is going to be way more entertaining," Brett said with a laugh.

"The joke's on you, *Brett*," she told him, hands on hips. "Because you're in the back with him if he's still dripping wet when it's time to go home."

Logan was almost rolling on the grass he was laughing so hard.

"On second thought, he won't be wet, because we'll be using your T-shirt to dry him," she said.

"I take it all back," Logan said, still smiling. "You guys are perfect together. I've never seen Brett bossed around like this—ever."

Jamie grinned, but she had to move fast when Brett burst into a sprint and hurtled toward her.

"Don't you dare!" she squealed, running as fast as she could to get away from him. "Logan, help!"

Brett grabbed her around the waist, almost knocking the breath from her, before tossing her over his shoulder and leaving her powerless to do anything other than try to kick him.

"Take me anywhere near that water and I'll kill you," she hissed.

"Oh, baby, I like it when you talk rough," Brett whispered, slapping her on the backside.

"I mean it, Brett. Logan!" she screamed for him to help her again, but he never came to her rescue. "Logan!"

"Hey, you told me not to interfere," Logan called out. "This is me not interfering."

"Bear!" she yelled. "Bear, help me. Get Brett. Get Brett now!"

The dog who was supposed to be impossible to get out of the water leaped out with as much gusto as he'd leaped in, his big bark echoing around the park.

"Good boy, Bear!" she told him, still upside down over Brett's shoulder.

Brett stopped moving and put her back on her feet, watching the dog as he wagged his wet tail and kept barking.

"Jamie?"

"Get him, Bear!"

Bear launched at Brett and knocked him to the ground, giant paws landing square on his chest before he took him down.

"Just licks," she told him. "Lick Brett."

Her dog did as he was told, and now it was her laughing, watching Brett pinned to the ground with Bear lying on top of him, soaking wet, pleading with her to make it stop.

"Who's wet now?" she asked.

Logan held his hand up for a high five, and she gave him one back. This was how it was supposed to be—Brett and Logan getting on like they always had. And she felt good. Ever since Sam had died, she'd been like a fish out of water, but all that had changed, and she couldn't have been happier.

"Come on, Bear, let him go," she commanded. "That's no way to treat your new daddy."

EPILOGUE

JAMIE LOOKED AROUND the large table and couldn't wipe the smile from her face. A year ago, she'd been a widow, and even her friends had struggled to know what to say to her, or how to treat her. And now? Now she was married to a man she could be herself with. A man who wasn't scared by the fact that she would always love the husband she'd lost, who was okay with her wearing her old wedding ring on her other hand, because Brett had loved Sam, too. Perhaps even as much as she had.

A tap on a glass made her turn to her new husband, eyes locking on his as he grinned and leaned sideways to give her a quick kiss.

"What are you doing?" she whispered to him.

"I'm about to do my speech, unless you want to go first?"

A speech? She hadn't even thought about speeches, had been so preoccupied with her vows that she hadn't even considered having to speak in front of everyone at the table.

She watched as Brett stood up beside her, their friends and family lowering their voices until they were eventually surrounded by silence.

"I guess I need to start by thanking you all for being here," Brett said, one hand holding his champagne flute, the other falling to rest on her shoulder. "This was a day we only wanted to share with those people closest to us, and there is one person that isn't here today that I would like to acknowledge."

Jamie reached for Brett's hand, her palm covering his fingers. She didn't want to cry, but the whole day had been so emotional and now she had tears caught in her lashes again.

"We all know I wouldn't be standing here today with Jamie if Sam was still alive," Brett began, taking a big breath before continuing. "Sam was my best friend, and I always promised that I would look after Jamie if anything ever happened to him. I know he wasn't meaning it quite so literally when he said that—" Brett paused as a few of their guests chuckled "—but I also know that he would have wanted us both to be happy in his absence."

Jamie stood then, needing Brett to know that she wanted to hear what he was about to say, what he was already saying, and not knowing how to. She looped her arm around his waist, holding him tight.

"Sam was the only one of us who was married, and no matter how much we teased him about marrying so young, we loved Jamie as much as he did. I just want to say, Sam, if you're up there—" Brett wiped his eyes with the back of his hand before holding up his glass "—that I will look after this woman until my dying breath."

Jamie had tears falling fast down her cheeks, curling into her mouth. There was nothing she could do to stop them, and she also didn't want to. Because she had loved Sam with all her heart, and now she loved Brett, too, just as deeply but in a different way. And she needed to hear what he had to say.

Brett turned toward her, putting down his glass and taking both of her hands into his.

"I always told Sam he was the luckiest

guy in the world, and I mean it when I say I will look after you. One day, I might have to give you back to Sam, because I don't want to be fighting him in the afterlife, but while we are here, on this earth, I will never let you down, Jamie. I will always be here for you, and I will do anything to be the husband you need me to be. I love you."

Brett wiped away the tears that had stained her cheeks, before leaning in and kissing her softly on the mouth. She put her arms around his neck and held on tight, not wanting him to stop, but the clapping and clinking of glasses around them forced the kiss to an end.

Even though her throat was choked up still and her eyes wet with tears, Jamie turned to face the table. She needed to say something, and they were *her* family, *her* friends. They were here to celebrate, and if they saw her cry it didn't matter.

"I don't have anything planned to say, and I'm sure you're all ready for dinner to be served, but I'd like to say thank you to all of you for being here today." Jamie looked at the light hanging above the table, needing a second to gather her strength and force her emotion back as best she could, so she could get the words out. Brett took her hand and squeezed, and it was all she needed to find the strength to continue. "When I married Sam, I knew I'd found my soul mate, but it seems that I'm one of the lucky ones." She squeezed Brett's hand back. "Brett was our friend for so many years, and now he's my husband. Life has a way of throwing us curveballs, some so bad that we wonder how we'll ever live through them, but Brett has proven to me that sometimes we have more than one soul mate in the world. I am so grateful to be standing here today, with the man I love."

Jamie reached for her glass and held it up. "To Brett, for being the love of my life, and teaching me that falling in love for a second time might be a miracle, but it was one that I deserved."

"To Brett." The words echoed around their table as everyone raised their glasses.

"I love you, Brett. So much," she whispered to him.

"And I love you, too, baby," he said, dropping a kiss to her forehead.

As they sat down, two waiters appeared

with the main courses, but it was the tapping against a glass again that had Jamie's attention, followed by a deep *huh-hmm*. She scanned the table and realized it was Logan, sitting directly across from them.

"I'll make this quick because dinner is being served," Logan said, standing. "For the past ten years, the two most important people in my life have been Sam and Brett. When Sam died, we were all hit hard, and thinking about Jamie being on her own was almost as hard as losing him." He gave her a wink across the table. "I might have given Brett a black eye when I first found out, but I honestly believe, now I look back on what happened, that Sam would have told me what a jerk I was being. Because looking at these two today, it's obvious they were meant to be together." He held up his glass. "And let's not forget Bear, Sam's loyal dog, who has taken up the role as Jamie's number-one protector. If anyone didn't approve, it would have been Bear, but even he seems to accept this union." Logan laughed. "To Brett and Jamie, two of my favorite people in the world."

Jamie smiled at Logan—the man who

had been her first husband's best friend and was undeniably Brett's best friend, too—and held up her glass. She took a slow sip before looking at every single person seated around the long table again. The white tablecloth was set with low candles from one end to the other instead of flowers, because she'd wanted to be able to see and talk to everyone, and she loved watching the smiles and chatter as she looked at them all now.

Brett nudging her broke her trance, and she switched her attention to him.

"You okay?" he asked.

"More than okay," she assured him, looking down at the plate of food in front of her.

"Then eat up, Mrs. Palmer," he said, waggling his eyebrows and making her laugh. "Because you'll need *all* your energy tonight."

Jamie elbowed him in the ribs but he was having none of it, swiftly grabbing her arm and pulling her in for another quick kiss.

"I'm so pleased I married you," he said, his mouth hovering over hers.

"Ditto," she said, laughing as he kissed the tip of her nose instead of her lips.

She reluctantly turned her attention back

to her food—king prawns, calamari and scallops tossed in her favorite linguine with garlic.

Life didn't get much better than this.

* * * * *

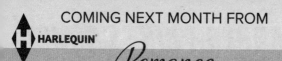

Enjoy this sneak preview of
STOLEN KISS FROM A PRINCE, the sparkling new
Harlequin Romance story from Teresa Carpenter!

"SO WISE." HE kissed the back of her hand, the heat of his breath tickling over her skin making her shiver, distracting her for a moment. The old-fashioned gesture was definitely not meant to be shared between employer and nanny. And then he turned her hand over and kissed the palm.

Her breath caught. *Oh, my.*

He regained her attention when he framed her face in two large hands and lifted her gaze to his.

"Thank you." His thumbs feathered over her cheeks collecting the last of her tears. "You are a very giving woman."

"No one should be alone at such a time." She lifted her right hand and wrapped her fingers around one thick wrist, not knowing if she meant to hold him to her or pull him free.

"It's a dangerous trait." The thumb of the hand she held continued to caress her cheek, though he seemed almost unaware of the gesture.

"Why?" she breathed.

"Someone may take advantage of you."

A knot clenched in her gut. Someone had. The harsh memory threatened to destroy the moment. She should step back, return to her duties. But she didn't. Because of the glint of vulnerability in his eyes.

Instead she bit her bottom lip and stayed put. For the first time she successfully shushed it. Perhaps because she needed this moment as much as he did.

HREXP0314

"There is only you and me here." She blinked, noting the look in his eyes had changed. The pain lingered but awareness joined the grief. "Are you going to take advantage?"

"Yes." He lowered his head. "I am." And he pressed his mouth to hers. He ran his tongue along the seam of her lips then nipped her bottom lip. "You tempt me so when you torture this lip."

She opened her mouth to protest, but he took full advantage, sealing her mouth with his. Heat bloomed, senses taking over